Lincolnshire Folk Tales Reimagined

Lincolnshire Folk Tales REIMAGINED

Edited by Anna Milon
and Rory Waterman

Five Leaves Publications
www.fiveleaves.co.uk

Lincolnshire Folk Tales Reimagined

Edited by Anna Milon and Rory Waterman

Published in 2025 by Five Leaves Publications

14a Long Row, Swann's Yard, Nottingham NG1 2DH

www.fiveleaves.co.uk

www.fiveleavesbookshop.co.uk

ISBN 978-1-915434-28-9

Printed in Great Britain

CONTENTS

INTRODUCTION

This book brings together new work in fiction and poetry that takes inspiration from Lincolnshire's wealth of folk tales. In all cases, however, the works are original compositions. Each author has also provided a note on his or her practice, and we have supplemented the stories and poems with a section of gloss notes on the original tales and sources.

All authors in this book have strong connections to Lincolnshire, and in some cases have lived in the county all of their lives; biographical notes can be found at the end of the volume. We selected several contributors early in the anthology's conception, and others through an open competition. Our selection process was influenced, in part, by a love of plurality: the book includes fantasy, crime and historical fiction, innovative and formally-intricate poetics, humour and sadness, old and new, here and elsewhere, and brings together writers with varied life experiences, backgrounds and influences, rolling all into a variety show bill.

Unlike in many other European countries, no systematic survey of folk tales in England was attempted in or around the nineteenth century, when it was noticed by the literate and literary classes of the time that so many folk tales (and customs) appeared to be dying out. Work of this kind was undertaken locally, usually by men of the cloth and wonderfully obsessed antiquarians, very many of them women. We have these people to thank for preserving many tales across the country, and in Lincolnshire they include the likes of Mabel Peacock and Marie Clothilde Balfour, both of whom lived in the north of the county, near Kirton in Lindsey. In the early twentieth century, their work was continued principally by people like Ethel Rudkin, who also lived close to Kirton for much of her life but who travelled far and wide, and the Reverend James Alpass Penny, who collected tales principally around Horncastle and Woodhall Spa. Rudkin, in particular, had a capacity to get in among her human subjects, as a true native and an easy conversationalist. But in many other cases, one wonders whether a local labourer or old lady or schoolchild might have self-bowdlerised when telling stories to the local vicar or a lady in a posh hat, and the extent to which some of those collectors might have altered the tales they heard to suit their own moral purposes. We cannot know what we have lost.

Some folk tales, nationally, were preserved during the first waves of tourism: wealthy tourists liked a tale, and tour guides liked a tip for telling one. But those tours tended to follow Romantic impulses, and headed to mountains, large lakes, waterfalls. We don't have those things round here. Lincolnshire was subsequently marginalised when some of these folk narratives clung on to, or made their way back into, our national conscience. Modern books about folklore in England tend to continue the trend and treat England's second biggest county – where old traditions persevered for longer than they did in most other places – as though it barely exists. The folklorists mentioned above are not widely known, even among scholars of folklore, and their books languish out of print. And yet many of the tales they recorded linger, quietly – often known very locally, if almost nowhere else.

We encourage you to go back to the originals, or to the inspirations, for these stories. Some reflect the prejudices of the times in which they were written or recorded, often directed towards Gypsies and other perceived outsiders, and towards women. (Modern times are also not without ingrained prejudices, of course, including mutations or continuations of those prejudices.) On the other hand, folk tales often have untraceably long lineages, and can have profound things to tell us about who we were, are, and might be, for better and worse. This book is testament to the power of those tales to inspire some of our finest living authors, writing in a bewilderingly broad range of styles – and to the ease with which many of them can be twisted into new shapes, as folk tales always have been.

The authors were given free rein to choose any tale or tales they liked, using the editors of this book as sounding boards if they wished, in addition to other resources such as the Lincolnshire Folk Tales Project online folk tale map. We asked them to take whatever liberties they liked to make the work their own. They could write in poetry or prose, or blend both, and were encouraged both to lean into their stylistic proclivities and push themselves in new thematic directions. We wanted them to inhabit the work, to make it their own, and then to give it to you fresh.

The storyteller and scholar of myth Martin Shaw provides a warning to storytellers, one this book frequently tests:

> The rule – and there is one – about old stories is
> that you can add a flavour here and there, but
> don't change the recipe completely. If you cut
> and paste stories together, the ancestral heft
> tends to drop out of the endeavour and you are
> left oddly weightless.[1]

There is a lot to be said for the gentle tweaking of tradition, and indeed for its wholesale preservation. But as there is nothing new under the sun, the art of writing itself is one of making new clothes from old materials. Every story is an old story, and every good new story is old story made new. However, this anthology is not primarily interested in telling old folk tales. There are partial exceptions: some authors have indeed kept close to the originals of an almost-forgotten tale, recovering it and reimagining it stylistically. Others, however, have joyously, sometimes impishly deviated at right angles from the original tales that inspired them. Yet others have made a new tale where they thought one seemed to be missing. And others still have brought more than one tale together into a new whole.

This anthology has been produced as part of the Arts and Humanities Research Council-funded project Lincolnshire Folk Tales: Origins, Legacies, Connections, Futures. We gratefully acknowledge the AHRC and Nottingham Trent University for their support. The Lincolnshire Folk Tales Project also benefits from partnerships with other organisations, including Heritage Lincolnshire, Adverse Camber Productions, Lincolnshire Life, the University of Lincoln and, last but not least, Five Leaves Publications.

---

[1] Martin Shaw, Courting the Wild Twin (Chelsea Green, 2020), p. 90.

DRAKES AND TITANS

Aliya Whiteley

After Father returned from the war he were not good for much, and then the Spanish Influenza came to Anwick and he rolled over for it without once thinking we might be better off with him rather than without him. Mother had it too, but nothing takes her without a good fight. She carried on washing other people's clothes, drying them in front of the fire, or in long lines in the garden, strung from wire, when it were not mizzling. I only wish she'd gone to take on the Hun instead, and the whole war would have been over much quicker.

I didn't have a thing, no cough, no fever. *Born lucky*, Mother said. And not a thing to show for years of schooling, either, nothing happens to me except William Pabody and his lot scragging me every lunch for my apple which was not so lucky however you look at it, and anyway, that's all in the past and now we are in the new decade of the nineteen-twenties, with summer near upon us, and I have found work with Mr Saunby the butcher. Saunby and Son, his shop is called, even though he has no son left to help him, so I will be paid to make the deliveries on the bicycle. Mr Saunby says I can have a day off every other Tuesday and take the bicycle to Sleaford if I like, to see the new picture house there. I might go, but I'm saving the bit of my wages that Mother leaves me. I keep it in the pewter tankard that used to be Grandfather's, then Father's, then came to me, and it sits on the shelf above my bed, in the back room. When I get enough I'll… well, I don't know just yet but I'm dreaming of different places to go and different things to be. I haven't told Mother yet.

There's talk in the village of having a memorial in St Edith's to the war's dead, and I feel the eyes of people upon me, gorming as I deliver their chops and sausages. They say to themselves: *Gerald Bardwell, not one of the dead then. A lucky young man.* No, I'm not one of the dead, and I never will be: I was saved by being too young, and now they say there'll never be another war and it's a new country for the next generation to lead. And sometimes I feel brave and true and able to do that, and other days I'm still squeamish about wrapping up the raw meat in wax paper before I set out on my deliveries, but Mother says I'll get used to it, and should let Mr Saunby teach me all he knows about the butchery business as that's a good living, and Mr Saunby has a soft spot for me now, having lost his own son. Sometimes when he looks at me I think he sees his boy, George, instead. George was two years older than me, and that was not so lucky.

I went along to Sleaford on the main road and sat in the picture house and had thoughts about asking a girl to go with me but there were something about being there in the dark, all closed in with the screen flickering and the people telling their stories without words, that felt wrong to me when there's so few men left who can do such a thing, so the next Tuesday

I told Mr Saunby I'd rather be leaving the bicycle and taking a walk about the fields around the village, maybe out towards Ewerby, and he said, "Have a sandwich with a bit of haslet to take with, then, duck," and I took my gift and headed out, thinking I'd maybe spot the first of the big dragonflies by the pond, zipping past – bright blue and green hunters they are. It was one of those days that makes you feel like summer is only one last breath of chilly wind away, and I cut along the back of Pabody's lands, where I could see his farmhouse in the distance: a big house with the two barns behind it. Everyone knows he keeps his horses in one and his Titan in the other, putting it away every night like it's an animal that needs to be fed and stroked, and locked up against the weather.

Farmer Pabody is right proud of that machine. He brought it into Anwick when he got it from a new company in Boston last year, and he stopped it in front of the County Forge, so Cradock the blacksmith ceased hammering and came out to stare, and everyone else did too. Pabody was sat up on the seat, his back very straight, and he announced it was called the Titan, and I touched one of the big red wheels but he gave me a look and I snatched my hand away. All the Pabodies are known for their tempers. Those wheels were the biggest I've ever seen, big enough to crush a man dead like one of those tanks at the front, and I could tell many people were thinking the same thing from the way they looked at it, but nobody said much. And then Pabody said that it could do the work of twenty horses or a hundred men, and he repeated it as if he'd been told it and he believed it, like we used to recite dates of wars past in school, so certain of it. I used to wonder why, if it was all so obvious and true, it needed endless repeating. Still, everyone started saying it, it was definitely true – twenty horses or a hundred men – and seeming impressed by it even though we knew what had happened to the hundred men it was replacing.

When I touched that wheel it was very cold, and it had none of the mud of the fields on it yet, but watching it at a distance on my day off, sandwich in hand, I could see that it had become a squaddy thing, a great churned up beast that reminded me of one of the big men without homes who used to travel the county and work the land, shuddering and breathing out into the sky.

I got closer and sat by a hedge, keeping my eyes on the Titan, and ate my sandwich, and tasty it was, too.

After a time, William Pabody came out of the barn – I was not close enough to see his face but I'd know his way of walking anywhere, rolling back on his heels with a strut, as I'd had plenty of experience watching for him across the schoolyard in the hope of keeping my apple for once – and he swung himself atop the Titan and started taking it down the dirt lane, over the squad from the rainspell day before last, churning up the brown water and flinging it from its path. It met the main road and steered to the right.

I felt a bit of jealousy, that I had a bicycle and that were only borrowed while William Pabody got to take that Titan wherever he wanted – but where would he be going? It were off his father's land, and I'll admit that's when curiosity got the better of me, and I stood up and started to follow at a trot, watching it trundle on as if it were in charge and William was only along for the ride. Perhaps it was going to the village, to sit in front of the forge again for admiration, but then it surprised me, taking a turn off the main road and heading for the common ground out behind St Edith's. There weren't much out there, except for the Anwick Stone, and that's when I thought: *no, no, he would not dare*, and my heart started hammering in my chest, my throat was tight, and I couldn't believe it but I knew I had to get there, even if I did get scragged again. So I ran straight for the stone, jumping the ditches, and I got there just as William had started throwing a chain around the thing to pull it from the ground.

The Anwick Stone. Here's the thing with that tale, I know it as well as I know myself, I've heard it many times from Mother. It were one of her favourites to tell when I was little and I asked for a story, last thing at night, but I can't say it was my favourite – I liked stories about brave men who went off to see something impressive, even if Mother said they usually ended up killing the impressive thing by the end. But I always wondered about the story because it were about Anwick, about the very place we live in and a thing I could see: that great stone out beyond the church, sticking up from the ground with that split in its crown, never to be moved. And men did try to move it, in the story, they tried and tried, and for good reason, too.
Mother used to say:

> *There is a stone that stands no distance from here. It always has and it always will.*

About the time of your grandfather's grandfather, the farmer of that field decided he'd had enough of the stone. He wanted to plough in a long straight line, and it vexed him that he had to steer around. And besides that, he had another thought in his head that he did not want to admit to; he had been told, as a boy, by his own grandfather, that the devil himself had hidden a horde of gold beneath that very stone, which made sense as there could be no safer place to keep wealth from human hands.

The farmer said to his neighbours: lend me your horses and your strength, help me move the stone, and I will buy ale at the Black Bull in Ruskington come Saturday, enough for us all and more besides. So the four men and eight horses set off to pull up the stone for good. But stones and trees both hold secrets, and that comes from the part of them that sinks deep into the ground. The oldest rule is: whatever reaches above, there's as least as much again that lies beneath. When the farmer and his friends roped the stone and set the horses straining, the stone only laughed at them, and settled itself deeper still.

Now, the farmer knew he looked like a fool in front of his neighbours, and worse, he had promised drink for them all, thinking he would be rich in gold. But it seemed he would be out of pocket and nothing but moithered, too, so he bade them to take off the rope and pick up spades, and they all began to dig.

They dug and dug around the stone, down and down, and they sang as they dug, old favourites they sang, 'Diggin' Torf Land' and 'The Poacher', and even a few hymns to protect them from the devil, so as would make the vicar proud. When they ran out of breath and stopped singing they heard a strange sound bubbling up from the ground, and when they put their hands on the rough old surface of the stone they could feel its amusement. It was laughing at them. They began to feel afraid and they would have stopped, but the farmer would not give up. He said to them: I'll buy ale every Saturday in this long summer, and so on and on and down and down they dug until the sun was setting and clouds came over the rest of the day, bringing rain.

This was not a mizzle but a devil-sent rain, siling down on the farmers, and it filled the hole in no time at all. The farmers could not scramble out, and they floated like water boatmen, lying on their backs and moving their arms and legs and going round in circles, with the top of the stone sticking up, an island in a great and growing lake. Maybe this entertained the devil for a time, but he soon grew tired of them all and sent a storm along, the thunder smashing and the lightning flashing so bold and bright that the horses all bolted for their warm dry homes. The devil wrote his annoyance in the sky over and over, building up to one almighty strike that hit the tip of the great stone and cluft it, just a bit, just enough to let out a golden liquid that did not stream down, or fall into the water, but stretched up into the air to make a fine line, a thread, that wrapped itself up into a shining ball. Then the ball grew a head and a tail, and sprouted wings to become a drake, casting its sharp emerald eyes over the land. Spying the farmers, it let out a loud squawk that left them all dazed, and they used the last of

*their strength to pull themselves from the water and run all
the way to the Black Bull, two miles and some.*

*When they reached the inn they stood before the fire,
soaked to the bone and shivering, and blurted out their story
to the amazed men within, who went out and searched the
skies for signs of that golden drake but never did find it. But
they did hear the laughter of the devil, long and hearty,
trembling the land, and from that time on everyone was in
agreement that they should not touch the Anwick Stone, not
even after the water drained and the land filled in around it
once more, no, for all sensible men know that we should
leave the oldest trees and stones in good peace.*

"Should you not be out on your bicycle?" said William Pabody,
looking up at me from fitting the chain around the stone. He
crossed his eyes, stuck out his tongue and pretended to steer
wobbling handlebars.

"Day off," I said. "What's this?"

"None of yourn. Pedal off." He took steps toward me, and
I thought maybe he'd move to scrag me, but when he got close
I could see he was not so much bigger than me anymore, not
like he used to be at school, and he was alone, too, without his
friends to help him. I could tell from his face that he'd realised
it too – for all I was the butcher's new boy and he was the
farmer's son.

The Titan was a different matter again. William returned
to it, and patted its wheel.

"You want to leave old stones in peace," I said.

"You don't believe all tha' old tale says?"

"Seems you do, if you think there's gold under there."

He shrugged. "Gold wouldn't be a bad thing."

"What do you and your father need gold for? He's the richest man around here!"

William shrugged, his eyes on the machine. "There's not so much money, and not so many men to work the fields come this time of year. He pays money to Crawford & Son in Boston every month for the Titan, and he says it's a lot to find so there's not pennies left over for good things."

I felt for him, then. Mother and I had been without much for a few years now, and I didn't think about it, but I remembered the shock when Father came back from the war and wouldn't work, would only sit in his chair by the fire, and all had to change around us.

"It's a fine machine," I said. I came to stand beside him and looked it over, my hands on my hips, like I'd seen the men look over sheep at the Sleaford market. I thought him seeing me admire it would make him feel better.

"It's grand for digging and turning over," he said. "Reckon it'll lift that stone, too, and if there happens to be gold underneath then it'll have earned its price many times over."

"What about the devil? Or the drake?"

"No such thing as drakes. Never seen one, never will." His eyes flicked up to the sky, then back to mine. "And not afraid of thunder nor lightning neither, nor of big puddles. I know better than to think a story can be real, and these are modern times and I have the Titan on my side." It was clear he was his father's son.

21

"In that case you'll not be needing me," I said, and made to turn away. He called my name, and I had to hide my smile.

"If you'd like to keep company, just to see the stone lifted, I'd understand it," he said. "And maybe I'd share a little of the gold, if there was any to be found."

"What, a share for me? To make up for all those apples of mine you took?"

William never was the blushing type, but he had the good grace to look a little ashamed at that. "School's a long way behind us now," he said, as if that was an apology. "We that are left should stick together."

"That makes sense," I said.

"Then you'll stay?"

I thought of what Mother would say if she found out I was behind this bit of foolery. But William was going to try to pull up the stone whether I kept him company or not, and he was right: we did need to stick together, us young men, and perhaps I'd be able to stop him from getting himself hurt. "I will stay," I said, and he beamed out a smile before hopping up on the Titan to get it started.

It raged into life easily: the loudest thing I'd ever heard. Surely everyone in the village were wondering what was making such a din. It made the earth shake as it moved off, taking up the chain, then pulling tight, tight, so the chain bit into the stone. But neither stone nor machine would win, that was how it looked; neither gave so much as an inch. I could hear nothing over the Titan, but I felt a groan come up through the ground, low and long. I could not bear the straining of the chain, so looked up at the sky, thinking to see clouds forming, a storm coming, but the day was still bright, the sun dazzling.

Then there was a glint of gold on the horizon, a flash – no, nothing, surely, but there it was again, blinding. It were a creature, a bird, moving fast towards us, and I put up my hand to shield my eyes from the sun to spy it better. I saw the wings, the curve of the neck. I recognised it, not from nature, not from life, but from those old stories, I knew it, and at that moment something hit me hard on the back of my head, a sudden shock that pitched me forward to my hands and knees, and I saw things I could not explain, and called out, "The drake, the drake," as its shadow skirled over me, cast me into darkness. William could not have heard me as the Titan strained on, but then it lessened, and ended its labour, and I was in sunshine again, dizzied and aching on the head, and I could hear my own breathing and the footsteps of William as he ran to my side.

"By god, it's done it," he said, and held out his hand, helping me to my feet. I looked around him, blinking to clear the spots from my eyes, and I saw the stone, dragged a distance away, leaving a trail of upturned mud and a deep gouge through the earth, ripped-up worms and soil laid bare to the sun.

"I saw it," I said. "I saw the drake. It were coming for us, right across the sky. And I saw…" I couldn't start to tell him.

"Don't be a born fool," said William. "It's done it!" He crossed the gouges to peer into the hole that was left, and I followed, and stood before it, and dared to look down to where the devil kept his treasure.

Nothing.

I say nothing – there was plenty in that hole, small things moving and crawling, spiders and ants and the mud sucking as it settled. But there was no gold. I thought of the drake, and of how golden it was, and maybe the treasure was the drake, flying away. All the gold was in the beating wings and beautiful neck of that drake, in the air and sky, and moving beyond our reach.

"We need to put it back," muttered William.

"What's that?"

"There's nowt there! Father'll leather me if he finds out I took the Titan and for no good reason. Help me, help me put it back." He ran to the place where the chain held the stone, and stopped, very still. I could not make sense of it. Then as I got nearer I saw it: there were two stones, not one. The Anwick Stone had split in two. It was as if some huge and terrible force had hit it, with a blow so strong that it had fallen into halves. I touched the back of my head and found a tender spot where a lump were already rising.

"There's no way to undo this," I said.

The day was as bright and windless as ever, but not a bird tweeted. I looked up, to the horizon, all the fields around. Everything was still. Frozen. Like a picture. Something rose in me, a sickness, and I bent double and spat on the ground.

"No, no, we'll put it back," William was saying, fiddling with the chain.

Two stones where one had been, and a golden drake loose on the world.

"We'll have to tell it," I said.

"What? No, no, we can…" He dropped the chain and slumped forward. It were no good; he could see it. Then he lifted his head and said, "We could go to the Black Bull, like in the old story."

It had a charm to it, as an idea, like something had come full circle, or it were part of an old tale and we had no say in what had happened. But it didn't feel like the right thing to me, not now. "The church," said I. "We'll go tell it at the church." And that is what we did, searching the sky for a drake and the land for a devil every step of the way.

By the end of that long day, at the start of summer, we had become the centre of the village's attention and near everyone of note had gathered to decide what to do with us. William and I were wise enough to keep our heads down and look penitent to the vicar and the blacksmith in particular. Even Mr Saunby cast me a bad look. But I had thought to get in worse trouble. Many folk just chuckled and said that it were the way of young men to do fond things thinking to become brave heroes, and nobody was in the mind to punish us for that. Mr Pabody said he'd have words with William later. He went back for the Titan and used it to move both parts of the stone to the front of St Edith's, putting them on the grass there.

A prayer was said, blessing the two stones made from one, and talk turned back to plans for a war memorial in the village, even though I couldn't see what those two things had to do with each other. Maybe the stones had got mixed up in people's minds: the old and the new, the whole and the split apart, and all the stones that had seemed firm and never to be moved, just like the stories that never changed from the time before.

While they had their talks, William sidled up to me and murmured, "You're not telling about the drake, then."

I shook my head.

"You think maybe it were a big bird, then? Buzzard, maybe?"

I thought about it, then said, "Reckon so."

He nodded. I noticed he had the start of a beard, and the skin on his cheeks were red, where it itched, no doubt. "Every other Tuesday your day off, you said? I sometimes have a Tuesday off, if you don't mind company."

"Depends," I said. "Will you bring me an apple?"

He nudged me, and I nudged him back. Not long after that the meeting ended and folk drifted back to their homes, their work, and all the things that they did day after day. No doubt William would get it from his father, but here's the strange thing: I almost envied him that, with only Mother's stern disappointment waiting for me at home.

Here's the thing: she'd already been told it all by Mrs Tabb, over the fence, and by the time I returned she only hugged me tight, and said, "Stay away from deep old stones and fast new machinery, Gerald Bardwell," and I said, "Yes, Mother," and helped her pick in the long lines of sheets she had managed to dry that day.

That night I sat by the fire while she ironed the sheets, and she said, "You'll make me wish I never told those stories if you're going to get in so much bother over them."

I looked hard at her face. I felt older and wiser, and she were very sad, I thought, pinched and worn and tired of worrying for me.

"How about I tell you a story instead?" I said.

"I'm listening."

I started to speak of what I had seen that day. At first the words would not come easily, but as I reached the part where the drake could be seen in the sky, heading for us, I found my voice and described its golden shine, and that majestic curve to it, so that it looked like dripping treasure brought alive. I spoke of the shadow cast over me, and the stone that cracked; how, at that moment, something hit me so hard on the head that I saw everything turned to shimmering water around me, the land swallowed by a lake, and not one Titan but many of them, all pulling, making waves as the roar of machines covered every bit of the earth. I spoke of how it felt like some evil had climbed from that split stone and made Lincolnshire his own, and nothing would ever be right again.

"What do you think hit you?" said my mother, only just loud enough to be heard over the thumping of her iron.

I tried to find my bravery – the courage that the folk of Anwick seemed to think I must possess, as a young man, but of which I felt none. "I think it was the devil himself," I said. "I think he smacked me as he passed and broke that stone for

27

spite, and we let him out, and it's our fault, isn't it?" I covered my face with my hands so she would not see me cry.

"Ah, give over," she said. "Don't waste much thought on that. There's more than one devil and they're always out and about somewhere, even in Anwick. Maybe people think the devils have been all used up in the war, over these last years, but that's not how it works. So they are present, and so are we, no matter where we go."

"I don't want to be a butcher," I said then, telling her the thing that made me most afraid. "I don't want to live my life in Anwick. I want to fly like the drake did. Far away. I didn't hate that drake, Mother. I wanted to be it. Rich and wild and free."

She stopped her ironing and looked at me straight. "Seems to me there's more chance than ever before for you to be what you want to be, son. And as long as you decide to keep living, I won't stop you. Working out how to make the most of your time. Finding out how what you want and what you fear come together – well, that makes for the best stories, doesn't it?"

And so it does. And so I still tell it, sometimes, and I think of Anwick, and the hole we left in the ground, and the vision I saw of a world of machines and monsters so fast in the sky, crossing to a future both rich and frightening, with the sea rising to swallow us all. I've seen both drakes and titans take over the world. I've travelled far. The old and new will fight, and break things in bits, and no doubt there will always be devils. But there will be stories, too. There will always be stories.

Author Comment

There are ancient stones dotted up and down the country and many have stories connected to them. They have long fascinated me, so I jumped at the chance to write about the Anwick stones, which I remembered from the time I lived in Ruskington about twenty years ago. I enjoyed recreating that landscape, as well as trying to give an old tale new life.

I wanted to find an aspect to the story that brought into focus the way that stories can create change in communities, so when I discovered that the stone(s) had been moved in the 1920s I decided to use that event as the focus of my retelling. I tend to plunge straight in as a writer, so I wrote a few openings from various perspectives, and settled on a voice that felt immediate and interesting to me, researching details of life in Anwick and Sleaford at the time as I wrote. It was a really engaging challenge; I worked to capture a personality that was right for the time and place, and hopefully did justice to a great tale of an old stone, and a local dragon.

GAP

Alison Brackenbury

County

Lincolnshire, my blank country. Maps, in space,
breed peas and sheep and villages. Each place
hides sorrow, story, its peculiar grace.

Gibbery Gap. Gibbery Gap.
Here come three women who pushed through the Gap.

'Mrs Brackenbury'
(as her neighbours would have addressed her, politely)
Mary
(1863-1913)

Long-widowed, short Victoria lingered on.
Mary, in a farm cart, reached Kirmington,
with six small heads beside her, Frank unborn.

All shepherds slept in damp straw at the Show.
John brought his ram's cup and a fevered glow.
Pneumonia. Antibiotics? No.

Do we risk drugs? Men dose pigs, crammed in sheds.
With all their home-reared bacon wolfed, no bread,
she faced the Parish Board. Frank, too, was dead.

The briskest farmer named the sum to give,
"That feeds the children. How am I to live?"
Clear-voiced, voteless. The gap. Do not forgive

what was snapped back, their east wind sharp outside.
"Young and strong enough to work! Woman, where's your
    pride?"
Mary washed farmers' sheets. They slept. She died.

"The older ones can mind the younger children."

The small fire whispered ash when Mary fell.
Each hedge slashed, she rushed home. Tall daughter, Nell.

'Miss E. M. Brackenbury'
(witness on her elder brother's death certificate)
Nell
(1894-1982)

The youngest thrived at Kirmington:
grave Fred, bright Walter who had sung

the Christmas play on winter's hills.
All sheets were boiled, Mary's chair filled.

'The Lady', costumed farm-boy, sang
"All I want is a nice young man!"

Kirmington's men marched thinned from war.
Nell, then a farmer's housekeeper,

passed their churchyard's chill empty grass.
Mary's first son, recruited, smashed,

shipped to Lincoln, died there. Like foam,
sloes whitened lanes, without Jack home.

She fought through thorns. She chose her past.
Eleanor May would cry at last

"We were so happy!" Stray shots show
her groom's greyed head, her startled glow.

The flower-decked niece Nell nursed once smiled,
gap-toothed bridesmaid, her missing child.

Small wars spring up from happiness.
Lost sister's husband? Scandalous!
What can joy cost? Forgetfulness,

our gap. When Armistice rang out
sailors with flu danced home from port.

One shepherd brother's breath would be
stopped by pandemic, horribly.
They hid his death from you, from me.

Mrs Rudkin
(1893-1984)

Past Long Lane's glint of may and moss
a woman strode. The village knew
her fame, her farmer husband's loss.
They swore he died in war. Untrue.
The Rudkins left her off his cross
where coils of churchyard bramble tossed.
He died in Lincoln's Gap, from flu.

Her ageing parents lived at war.
Off she went in her motoring cap.
She fought for pensions, bought her car,
her county glittered on the map.
She found adventures, gay and wild,
kept wedding flowers, had no child.
New marriage would take all. The gap.

She dug pots. A researcher came.
The journals failed to print her name.
Careful, she wrote all stories down.
Careless, he mentioned one he found.

Note: widowed in 1918, Ethel Rudkin, known informally as Peter, became a
    pioneering archaeologist and 'folklorist'.

Before
(a vicar, near Kirmington, counts servants for the 1911 Census)

In peace, in Brocklesby Rectory,
its teenage housemaid dusts stairs well.
Their Oxford son drives home for tea.
Long apron sweeps. She greets the bell.
Does he match smiling courtesy,
their laundress' calm daughter, Nell?

After
(letter to Mrs Rudkin, 1930)

Near Kirmington, Charles Phillips finds
a minor barrow. Lacking grace
(though he will rule at Sutton Hoo),
he writes that 'a native of this place'

pursues him. Mr John Johnson
(with weak heart and no veteran's cap)
survives to run Oxford's great Press.
The Rector's son knows Gibbery Gap.

Lost

Who will reach back? Not my grandfather, Fred,
prize shepherd of the Grange, off Caistor Lane,
who slices swedes while longwool rams are fed.

Who will recall? The waggoner's wife. For when
she lives in Kirmington, she chants a rhyme,
softened, as a neighbour says, for children.

Who will tell us this story? Irene Harris,
typing by a morning's brilliant screen,
for strangers, straight from Kirmington, with kindness.

Rhyme

Did 'Micklow Hill' boast a wealthy farm
where Walter's Plough Jags lined up, flushed and warm?

Our Civil War stays lost in frost and night.
Did Fairfax or a cornered captain fight

near Kirmington, in East wind? Dyke and wood
watched one man stumble down as best he could,

torn apart. Had he reached pain's last trance
where horses dropped, slow-motioned, like a dance?

'All the rest is lost', writes Irene Harris.
Did a man who butchered pigs write this?

'From Micklow Hill to Gibbery Gap
he carried his puddings in his cap.'

The Royalist, in high hat trimmed by feather,
or shepherd's cap, to keep off wind and weather,

staggered towards the village till he fell.
Was his home there? Sister or sweetheart? Nell?

His broken body doubled through the hedge,
crossed Caistor Lane, then crumpled at its edge.

That hedge still mourns. Young shoots, although March glows,
fall back into the cold clay. Nothing grows.

You will not find it on your back-lit map.
Gibbery Gap. Gibbery Gap.

Then

Between our promise and their truth, the gap,
with red leaves under Army boots. When blasts
shatter a drone commander's trusted walls,
head downhill through the old gap. There at last

soldier, in our next brief wars, she falls.

Echoes

How straight they stood! Let low times honour them:
Mary, who sang out truth to powerful men,

the sons her village cradled, like an arm.
"Lovely men. So very quiet. And calm."

Nell, without mother, baby, beaming groom,
a little stooped, in our cramped village room

tall as a flame, leaned with her kiss. And yet
the youngest brother, whom I never met,

Walter, whose wife feared Kirmington's dark time,
saved by his woodshed, sang the Lady's rhyme.

'Lady's' Song
(from a Kirmington plough jag)

I am a lady bright
and fair my fortune
is my charm, its true
that I've been borne away
from my dear lover's
arms. He promised for
to marry me as you
will understand, he
listed for a soldier
and went into foreign
lands...

The Recruiting Sergeant marches, in a village veteran's red.
He reaches to the Lady. She chooses the Fool instead.

Land

The hedge has lost each lark to winter wheat.
The clay, left airy under horses' feet
lies crushed for cheap food no one can afford.
We cannot sell our finest ram abroad.

Now

Where Kirmington and Grasby roads still meet
go where the red haws blacken under feet
listen where our children come to see

Gibbery Gap, Gibbery Gap
Gibbery

Author Comment

I have written, published and broadcast poems for most of my rushed adult life. Eventful subjects/distractions included family, horses (an inherited passion) and manual work. I used to say, idly, that 'one day' I would write, in prose, of the extraordinary Lincolnshire village where I grew up, as a descendant of skilled, silent servants and shepherds. There I knew and visited the legendary 'Peter' Rudkin, the great folklorist. A pandemic had killed Mrs Rudkin's soldier husband, and my shepherd great-uncle in 1918. Our own pandemic of 2020 did not kill me, but in its desolation I found myself, mentally, back in the village.

'There are so many stories', a fellow-writer said. I knew many village stories. I found more. Victorian witches; the Weatherhoggs (clever bike-menders and saddlers); Emma, whom Mr Weatherhogg pushed home from the pub every Saturday – in a wheelbarrow. I have written this book once: *Village*, which is forthcoming. That is the archive version – all the scandalous great aunts, lost children of 'Singlewomen', playground rhymes, names of horses that ploughboys called at dawn across Lincolnshire fields: 'C'up! C'up!'

That book is too long. As I drafted, and now re-shape it for final revision, I have written only the occasional poem which banged with exceptional fury at my door.

I found too many gripping stories from villages outside my own, for Lincolnshire, like other counties, is a living web. My shepherd grandfather grew up in a village called Kirmington, where war and flu swept away two strong brothers. Through hints from Mrs Rudkin, and present-day kindness from Kirmington villagers, I found a brutal legend from another war. And so I came back to poetry, writing of memory – and of deliberate forgetfulness. Kirmington's folktale of 'Gibbery Gap' survived in just one couplet. I hope, in my re-telling, to put the 'folk', the almost-silenced villagers, back into their story.

THE HOOD

Alex Harvey

I.

There was something in the water.

Bronwen had been spear-fishing all morning, sent out before dawn to fetch food for the camp. But there were no fish. She had gone to sleep late the night before – her fault – but there had been visitors to the settlement with news to share about men in shining armour, men with red plumes, men who fired whistling flames out of their hands. Bronwen had been captivated by such tales; these were new visitors to Prydein, the first visitors since the Age of Ancients when her ancestors had wrestled this land from the clutches of giants. "Thank you for your good fortune, Beli," Bronwen muttered, then she made a short dance and flicked her spear to the luck god who dwelled in the earth somewhere nearby. There were a few roundhouses near Beli's forest: a sacred place for sacred people – the others weren't welcome there apart from at midsummer. Summer was a long way off, and as Bronwen peered through the ice-cold water looking for spinefish, she wished she was somewhere else, somewhere sun-kissed.

During one of these daydreams, she had spotted the thing floating in the water. She was on the edge of the archipelago, from where she could see land rising in the distance. The River Treanta dawdled before her. This was the furthest she had ever walked from the village. Older settlers had warned her not to come over here, they said it was filled with the souls of the restless dead, but Bronwen had not believed them, her mind occupied by more tangible fears. There had been a battle a week before between the Coritani tribe and the people who lived on the other side of the River Ambra. Her lover, Boggfael, had sailed over to meet them in a reprisal. How she wished he would come home, sweep her off her feet with tales of daring-do, gift her with tributes, and set everything back to how it should be. Most of all, perhaps, Bronwen wanted a baby.

But instead of new life, she was faced with a dead body, brown and leathery, stuck beneath the surface of the water like a trapped demon. Bronwen wished she had listened to the warnings of the old women in the settlement; she remembered fragments of last night's conversation: *there are mud hags over there… witches cursed a man, left him as a swamp fiend… souls are trapped down in the dirt, wisps on the wind.*

The air was still, breathless. Bronwen was frightened, peering into the eyes of an unspoiled, expressionless corpse. He looked ancient, and was dressed in peculiar clothing: he wore no metal, no accoutrements, but was wrapped in cloth and leather, with a hood round his head.

Suddenly, something came over her. In these ever-changing times, the village needed something powerful, something dark, something from the past to cling to. Beli and the good fortunes were clearly not enough, especially if new shining enemies clad in crimson and bearing an eagle standard were approaching from the south. The body made the water bubble slightly, and for the first time all winter, Bronwen saw fish in it. She did the unthinkable, and reached out.

When she returned home, the settlers were surprised not by the amount of fish she had over her shoulders – although that was impressive and abnormal in winter – but by the hood she wore. Bronwen revealed it had come from a water spirit, who had summoned innumerable fish from the depths to feed the village.

She was to be amazed in turn. Bronwen had been out all day, and while she was encountering that mire revenant, Boggfael had returned home with treasures, tributes, tales. "Let us make a baby," she said to him, after much celebration. "And let us remember this day. And celebrate it forevermore. It will certainly make winter bearable!"

Everyone agreed with that, even the old crones. Every winter, they would remember the incorruptible hood sunk beneath the water, and the good luck it had brought them. They would dance around the fire and pass it back and forth, all sharing a touch. Maybe this island had been a good place to settle after all.

II.

Many years ago, a king had died here. They said his name was Edwin, or maybe Oswald. Ethbert couldn't remember which was which. He couldn't remember who the current king was either. His great-great-great grandfather had fought in a war not too far from here, out in the heath-field. That was where Edwin had died – or was it Ethelfrith? All the names of those northerners from over the Humbre sounded the same. Ethbert lived on his island and he didn't like being bothered by the comings and goings of kings. Kings weren't welcome here unless they had been born here. Ethbert tried to tell his grandson that *they* used to be kings here, tried to tell all his children this, but they weren't interested. Times were changing.

From the south came tales of fire and destruction. Men went off to fight and never came home. Ethbert had fought his fair number of battles, and his knees would no longer let him. He traced the lines of scars up and down his body. His first, a cut along his jowl, had been given to him by one of the Lindsey-men to the east, vile barbarians who lived in the uplands far from the river. His second scar, originally a deep gouge in his side that had subsequently been filled with cobwebs, was from a spear thrust by a Northman. The Northmen were all over the place now, but Ethbert held no grudges. He had never had a problem with the ones who had settled here, led by their man Hakr.

Hakr had been a strapping giant of a man, a behemoth from a land he called 'Rogafjord' over the sea. He had come here as a humble farmer, a retired warrior, with about three hundred of his finest soldiers, and women – Ethbert's second wife among them. That was years ago now. Hakr had since died, but his farm remained. Almost overnight, he had turned an empty hill into a bustling market, and still that market bustled.

Ethbert had lost many people over the last few years, since King Alfred had died to the south. He didn't remember who the king was now, just that there had been a mighty war fought between some of Hakr's friends and those people from Wessex, and now Alfred's son (or was it daughter?) was riding north with a great army to claim territory for their kingdom.

Some of Ethbert's sons spoke the *Donsk Tunga*, the Danish Tongue. Others spoke English. Many spoke both. Their bloodline was a web that held the North Sea together – people from the Isle, yes, but also people from that faraway land called Frisia, and from Juteland and Rogaland.

Suddenly he heard faint battle noises. That had always been familiar to Ethbert, and to his father, who had fought against pirates. His great-great-grandfather had saved a king from a spear-throw once – Edwin? Oswald? Ethbert didn't know. *His* father had fallen in battle near the River Idla, by the ball-shaped tree just south of the Isle. Ethbert always looked to his ancestors for support.

Here, at Hakr's old farm, he had collected a stash of relics from the many kings who had tried to claim his territory. There was continental gold, knotwork from Scandza, amber from Constantinople, pottery from Rome, black feathers from a raven, a pendant of Odin's face. And a crusty leather hood. The highest treasure of all was locked in a small wooden box, a reliquary. Ethbert and the Isle shamans only opened the box at Midwinter, during the twilight festival. Contained within was a piece of a dead king – Edwin, or Oswald, or maybe Ethelfrith, he wasn't sure. Legend had it that where the king had fallen a holy spring had emerged, and an eagle had torn off his arm and flown it over the Isle, dropping it above the spot where Hakr would build his farm. Ethbert hadn't looked at the finger for a while but he remembered it, silver and gleaming.

"Want to see something from your history?" he asked Bjorn, his fifth son's second son, and Bjorn nodded. He had that foreign glimmer about him; you could tell his mother had been a shieldmaiden in her youth.

Ethbert opened the box and shared the tale. Then he shared all his memories of those Midwinter festivals – the Islonians dancing round a fire, passing the arm of a king between them, symbolically re-enacting the battle.

But yes, times were changing. Ethbert just hoped that history would remember him, and Hakr's farm, and the tall tales of dancing round the fire.

III.

Lady Elizabeth missed home. Home was a warm hearth, a serving boy called Charlie, the hunting dogs of the palace grounds. Home was Castle Hedingham, her mother and father, the inherited fortunes of the Earls of Oxford. Home was riding horses in the sunlit forests, through the babbling brooks, over the rolling uplands. Home was down south: warmer, kissed by the sky – and, crucially, not here. Here was wet, cold, miserable. Here, the only colours were those worn by Elizabeth: red, ruby, crimson, a silk hood. The colours of Elizabeth de Mowbray – but how she hated that name!

She had never wanted to marry again. Her first husband, but not her first love, had been Sir Hugh. Eight years they had lived together, down by the sea in Devon, where they had raised their son. At least *he* was still alive, though Elizabeth worried about how he was faring in France, fighting the good fight. Sir Hugh had succumbed to the plague about a decade ago, but the wound this had left in her was still fresh. He had been a good, virtuous man, one of the founding members of the Order of the Garter. That was why she had fallen in love with him – not because of his achievements or wealth, but because of his devotion to helping others. 'Chivalry, my dear' had been one of his most frequent phrases. Elizabeth had found it corny at first, though deeply charming, not that she had ever told him so. In the end, it had been her father's wishes that brought them together, but she hadn't regretted it. And since he had passed, all she could do was remember Hugh's gallantry, how he'd chase her down the lane to return her belongings if she'd forgotten them before a ride.

Elizabeth looked over her shoulder now, half expecting to see his memory and a different sky. Instead, she saw her new husband's procession in the distance, unable to ride as fast as she was doing. She was the only colour on the hill. Everything else was shrouded in a thick pea fog. She could hear the sounds of the place: waterfowl beating overhead, the ribbet-ribbet of frogs, the lapping of strakes on water, the occasional breach of a bog-fish, and the unintelligible drawl of the locals.

Elizabeth now lived on the Isle of Haxeholm, some backwater estate belonging to John, her second husband. She didn't understand John. He owned a wide crescent of lands from the Yorkshire Moors to the coasts of Old Anglia – he was wealthy, *very* wealthy, which was perhaps the only good thing about him. Despite this, John spent all his time in this wet, cold wasteland; the rest of his estate was in the care of his litany of sons, the devil-spawn of his previous wives. The people spoke almost no English, and spent their time performing bizarre pagan ceremonies: they danced around a smoky fire every Midwinter, and went to war with one another over pieces of dangled history.

Elizabeth barely saw John during the day. Still, she had to perform her womanly duties. A lack of love didn't stop John from entering her bed every night. She just wanted to get away, to ride and ride and not look back.

She heard her husband's servants call to her from the bottom of the hill, urging her to return, so she spurred her horse onwards and raced into the mist at the top of the hill, which crested out into a small cluster of farms called Acheseia. Muck-covered mud-men ploughed the fields and barrel-dwellers hoisted crates of sea serpents over their backs. Their world was a grey one, a brown one, and they certainly did not expect to see the red streak of embroidered silk and gilded jewellery pass them by that morning. In Devon, Elizabeth had initially looked down on the poor, but her first husband had shown her to support their inferiors. One of the tenets of the Order of the Garter was to give alms, land, food. And John *does* have a lot of land, Elizabeth thought. She wondered if she could sway him into donating some of his estate to the poor of Acheseia.

The mist had started to clear a little. She realised she had stopped when her husband's servants caught up with her. They said it was time to return home, m'lady.

"One moment," she said. Because here on the edge of

Acheseia was a small boy, covered in muck, dazzled by the radiant woman's finery. The boy waved. Elizabeth remembered Hugh in that moment, and saw in the boy's face the face of their son. She unclipped a strip of ruby cloth from her hood, and handed it to him, and he took it, gingerly, silently. Let that be the first gift, she thought. Elizabeth would sway her husband, and perhaps some of this empty land could be gifted away. It was the right thing to do.

As she rode off, the young lad gripped onto that piece of cloth as if his life depended on it.

IV.

"So, what is the reckoning?" asked Gilliam – who preferred to be called Gill – as his hands passed over the fire between him and Hilbert – who preferred to be called Hil.

"I think I will enjoy it," he replied, in a thick accent.

Hil spoke awkwardly because his folks had come from over the sea as drainers a few years back. He had met Gill, a local boy, in the market not long afterwards. At the start, they hadn't seen eye to eye: Gill was a swamp dweller and Hil and his folks were taking all that away. But, maybe a year ago, the lads had realised they had more in common than they'd first realised. They had stumbled across one another at the same fishing spot. Gill generally went at the week's end, Hil midweek, but it had been a stressful time for both, what with the canals being dug, so they'd both started coming here more frequently, to get a bit of peace and quiet, and had bumped into each other.

"You can't be 'avin this place. Get gone you! This place is mine!" Gill had shouted.

"Well I came here first. 'An I ain't leaving either."

That quarrel had continued for some time, till they both became distracted by something in the water. They had come for stickleback, pike, trout, but instead what had floated down the brown mire, thick with reeds and tangled roots, was a block of water-stained wood, half-rotten. A small crate. It approached the shoreline and came to rest against the mud. Gill and Hil had both looked at it, and both sets of hands had tugged it further ashore. Locked within – though there was no lock, and the wood pulled apart like wool – had been some sealed bottles. Some sodden paperwork too, but their eyes were on the drink.

"Wine, I think. French wine," said Hil, and then he'd uttered something in his own language, half-understandable to Gill, whose grandparents had taught him a bit of the marsh tongue just as the rivers had started to thin, shortly before they'd died.

"How is it you know about French wine?" Gill had asked.

"I once knew a couple Frenchmen back home."

Then Hil realised he didn't have anything to open the bottles with, though the local boy had a small leatherworking knife. Hil extended his hand for it, and Gill grudgingly obliged.

Hil cut right through the neck of the bottle without shattering it. How do you do that? Then came the pungent smell of France, where the sunlight was yellow and the fields were green, where the women were beauty and the food was joy. Hil had taken a swig, careful not to cut his lip, then passed it over, and got to work opening another.

They had got to know each other that night. "Where are you from?" Gill had asked.

"Friesland, o'er sea. It's like here, not too different. Lot of fish. Lot of Frenchmen too." Gill had laughed at that. But his own origins were less interesting: his family had lived here in the marsh for as long as he knew.

"Will we be hurt?" asked Hil, and Gill was suddenly brought back to the present predicament. The two lads were sitting on dry rocks near a hill, and there was a growing sense of community around them – people from the farms and hut clusters were coming over. Dutchmen, Frenchmen, local men, Isle-men, swamp men. They had all come to hear the Fool speak and to start the celebration that had been going on since Gill's grandmother's time, if not earlier.

"So, where will you go now?" asked Hil, always with the questions. Ever since they'd become drunkenly acquainted, Gill had been bringing Hil up to speed on local practices and traditions. They had a lot in common already, coming from similar swamps – separated by a sea, of course – but this peculiar festival, centred around the village of Achsey, struck Hil as one of the most interesting things he had ever heard of. It was bizarre, he pondered, as a brightly-coloured man with a soot-blackened face jaunted past. Apparently, it all had something to do with a queen, or a princess, who once lost her shoe in the village only for it to be returned to her by some trustworthy locals. Or was it about a dead king's arm? Or head? Hil wasn't sure; Gill had told him so many contradicting versions.

"We go to the fire now," ordered Gill, jumping to his feet, and polishing off the last of the ale – not French wine, sadly. "We shall go together, if you will?"

"I am glad of your company, and the ale, eh!" Together, they lumbered over, knocking shoulders with some of the lads from Kroll, who were said to be even more swampy than everyone else. Hil was sure Kroll was a new village, founded by his relatives from Friesland, but Gill's grandparents had said they had been to Kroll many decades ago, and that it had always been there, even before the water had started to lower.

A shame, thought Gill, that the marshes were receding. He didn't know it, but this would be the last festival at Achsey to take place within sight of the swamp water. It was soon to be gone entirely, on the orders of the King, and Hil's parents had been helping the drainage, but Gill didn't begrudge his new friend. Times were changing. They said soon the Isle would be home to even more new people. At first, that had scared Gill. But if these newcomers were anything like Hil, then the more the merrier.

V.

"Hoose agen hoose, toon agen toon, if a man meets a man knock 'im doon, but doan't 'ot 'im!"

The tenor of the speaker's voice interrupted the raucous assembly: a moshpit of drunkards, hooligans, youths, all scrambling for a bit of action. It was the sixth of January, and not ideal weather for a scrum, but you take what you get on the Isle. Dissatisfied, disillusioned, disappointed young men. Angry. Itching. Raring to go.

"*House against house, town against town, if a man meets a man knock him down, but don't hurt him.*" The over-thickened accent and dialect was merely the self-parody of an isolated rural drawl, a non-committal attempt at drudging up something folkloric from the deep past. The speaker was a normal smartphone-tethered twenty-first-century man, like all the others in the audience, including Boggs. Not all of them were listening.

Boggs was probably going to hurt people tonight.

Christmas, a miserable affair, had come and gone. There just wasn't enough money going round to do anything. They'd had cold meat and chips the day after, standard fare, nowt special. Now in his fifties, Boggs felt that he was getting old. It was the same each year. The same farms, the same tractors, the same interminable shifts up at the steelworks. The same soot, the same ash, the same beer from the fridge when he got in. The same snap for work every day, the same scran on the table when he got in. The same mates down at the pub, the same routine day in, day out, but less and less money coming in, more and more bills going out. Boggs was tired. It was *their* fault, them ones up top, shadowy figures down in London, those in charge of bills, banks, you name it. When Boggs had been a young lad, he'd wanted to make a name for himself down there, get smart and get rich, but the temptations of mucking about at the back of the class, smoking, drinking, laughing, had been all too great to ignore, and then he'd needed to bring in some money. Had he thrown it all away? Maybe. Whatever.

Boggs was brought back to the present by the smell and sight of black smoke. Yes, he was probably going to hurt people tonight. The speaker was Ade Garton, but tonight Boggs knew him as the Fool. Everyone in the crowd did, all here for the Haxey Hood.

The rain had started to pour, cold and steady. A beer jacket helped. Someone had lit the inaugural fire in damp hay behind the Fool, as someone did every year, and as it billowed the same old speech was being made. For a moment he was being transported elsewhere, away from here, to a different life.

He drained his beer, and then looked for a bin. In the past, everyone had lobbed empties over the heads of others. Couldn't do that now – health and safety gone mad. Much *had* changed, but for the most part the Haxey Hood remained dependably the same as ever, an immutable tradition at the heart of the Isle. Boggs couldn't help but feel proud of that.

Then the crowd started to surge to the right, towards the field where the game would begin, and as it did Boggs occasionally caught glimpses of a leather baton, the Hood: symbolic, but worth scrapping over. He locked eyes with a few of the lads from his school years, trapped here like him. A few old friends, a few old foes. Like him, they had lived on the Isle all their lives, and they were steelworkers now, or farm workers. Their fathers had been local and their fathers' fathers had been local.

Someone lit a flare. Someone else went to stop him. A thick cheer rose from the expectant crowd, itching for some action. Leering laughter followed a young lad in a hoodie as he was dragged away to the back of a van, his eyes lost behind his black goggles. Been there, done that, thought Boggs.

Up the road he walked, up road everyone walked, atop the hill to the water tower, atop the hill to kick it all off. He hadn't yet decided what team he'd be on. He supposed it didn't really matter in the end, just so long as it was the winning one.

There was something new in the corner. Well-dressed people with cameras, buffeted by the wet wind, wearing oversized ponchos. They hunched at the back of a clean van, wellies up to their shins. A logo Boggs had seen on the telly was emblazoned across the side.

"Nowt worth filming round here, love," he shouted over, and one of them gave him an awkward smile. Why were they here? But there was no time to think. Boggs looked over his shoulder at the growing anticipation, the swirling mass of warm bodies, huddled together to escape the rain, as the Lord held up his hand and declared the game afoot. Then he threw his cup at someone's head and rushed in.

Author Comment

The Hood is an original tale, or concatenation of tales, loosely based around an existing folk tradition from the Isle of Axholme. This is the Haxey Hood, the origins of which are murky, and the upkeep of which is dependent on the toil of hundreds of devoted locals from across the villages of Haxey and Westwoodside, and beyond. Pictures of the Haxey Hood usually dominate any Google search of the 'Isle of Axholme', and rightly so. Allegedly, in Late Medieval times, Lady Mowbray dropped her hood whilst riding near Haxey. A person from a nearby farm found it, but was too embarrassed to return it, so instead someone else took on that quest and was rightly rewarded. The initial discoverer was forevermore dubbed 'the Fool', and the winner awarded with land and estates. Lady Mowbray found the whole affair so delightful that she demanded it become an annual tradition. If you ask me, this is a bit too twee to believe, and while I am sure there are kernels of truth in it, I suspect the real origins of the Haxey Hood lie elsewhere. We will likely never be able to work out the exact origin of this event, in which two villages battle it out for a metaphorical 'hood' to hang in a pub of their choice, but it has parallels with much older fertility rituals. In any case, in order to avoid anything concrete, my tales instead focus on the ambiguity of history, the diversity of folk tradition and cultural elements, and the fact that many 'ancient traditions' are simply reworked time after time to serve new purposes.

THE BELVOIR WITCHES
THE NOT SO DAMNABLE PRACTISES OF THE FLOWERS OF BOTTESFORD

Jane Simmons

When the Flowers women work at the castle, the servants say they are
    too loud,
they pinch, they pilfer, they blaspheme, they perform lewd acts, bewitch
the men behind wives' backs, give kisses for free, and cunt for coins.
There's more besides – the cow has dried, the hens won't lay, the crops

are rotting in the fields. Mistress must turn them from the house –
turn the key and bar the door, and never see their faces more.
The Countess dithers for fear of their cunning, then buys them off
with forty shillings and adds on a bolster. A mattress too.

The servants snigger *they've made their bed, let them lie on that,*
and open their legs to earn their keep. The Flowers protest they've done
their best, but when the Countess will hear no more, they curse her
as they leave her door. The Earl and Countess soon fall sick; one

son dies and then the other – heir and spare – and there's no sign of
    another
to take the place of either. The Rutland family line is dead!
Who brought such trouble on their heads? The servants say: *remember*
the curse. This is the Flowers' vengeful work. Those women are witches

through and through. Evil roosts beneath their roof, their chimney smokes
the devil's breath, we've seen them fly across the moon, we've seen them
dancing, prancing naked in the woods, and jigging widdershins
round the church. Arrest all three! Arraign the lot. And so it's done.

All along the road to court, sticks and stones and worse are thrown.
The good wives hiss and spit. Old Joan protests her innocence, and asks
for holy bread. No witch is she, she will not choke, by Father, Son and
    Holy Ghost.
She takes one bite – oh no! – the blessed Host sticks in her throat.

The more she coughs, the more she chokes, and soon the witch is dead.
Pity her daughter Philippa, pity her daughter Margaret,
for now they go in fear of water, dead if they sink and
dead if they float. They fear the rope, they fear the fire, they fear

the wooden door, the rocks. What makes the innocents confess?
Is it a chance to save themselves? Our Mother was the guilty one –
she sold her soul for evil arts, the gifts of flight and second sight,
black Rutterkin the cat. She slept with Satan in her bed,

she suckled devils at her breast. We did the same but aren't
to blame – we only did as we were bid, we only did
our mother's work. She killed the first son with his glove – we only
stole it, nothing more. She lit the fire, boiled water in the pot,

she was the one who wore the glove and stroked the cat,
and she the one who sang the curse. Why not confess? We're dead
if we do, and still dead if we don't – the outcome's the same.
Yes, blame is shame – but could be fame. Joan sang her curse – she sang

it once, she sang it twice, she sang it thrice. And we, her daughters,
    both joined in!
We all sang once, we all sang twice, we all sang thrice – and lo, the deed
was done. The spell wound up, the son fell down, and when the second
son was dead, we cursed the Rutlands' marriage bed by burning
    feathers

and boiling blood. Yes, that was how we stopped their line for good.
Yes, we confess this wickedness, this wickedness we did not do.
So, hang us high from castle walls, and bury us without the church –
but when, in time, you all have died, then we will have the last word inside:

Francis Manners, Earl of Rutland who married þe lady Cecila Hungerford,
by whom he had two sons, both of which died in their infancy
by wicked practises and sorcerye

THE LINCOLN IMP

Jane Simmons

The devil, bored and in frolicsome mood,
sent down two imps to get up to no good:

"Dance widdershins around some churches,
and knock a few bishops from their perches."

In Chesterfield first, they twisted the spire
but they soon set their sights a whole lot higher –

Lincoln Cathedral could offer much more,
so they blasted open its great west door,

knocked down the dean, sent him arse-over-tit –
and that jape was only the start of it!

They tripped the proud bishop, who struck his head
and lay on the chancel floor as if dead.

They taunted the vergers and teased the choir,
then set the stone gargoyles to spouting fire

by tearing up hymn-sheets to set alight,
and adding prayer books to keep the blaze bright.

God's bones and blood – what a splendid joke,
two knaves fill a nave with soot and smoke!

They smashed stained glass, they put out the lights,
they provoked the choristers into fights.

Communion wine? Why, they drank the lot –
and then used the font for a pissing pot!

When an angel came down to warn the pair off,
they just answered back, "No, you can fuck off

or we'll pluck the fine feathers from your angel wings
and strike your halo so hard that it rings!"

Now, this was too much for the angel to bear,
"That's enough from you – you impudent pair!"

And with that, he turned the first imp to stone
and condemned him to spend Eternity alone

on the naughty step – only rather higher,
atop a pillar in the Angel choir.

The second imp fled, he took to his heels,
but the nave soon echoed to his outraged squeals

as the angel beat him all black and blue,
then turned this scoundrel to limestone too,

and set him up high on an outside wall
to sit out time through snow, storm and squall,

and that's where the imp still sits and grins
though shat upon daily by peregrines.

LINCOLNSHIRE HARES

Jane Simmons

The hare, the scotart, the bigge, the bouchart,
hares nose-to-tail round the bowl of the wolds –
the wei-beterem, the ballart, the go-bi-ditch, the soillart.
At Bolingbroke Castle there's a glimpse, a start, of
the wimount, the babbart, the scot, the deubert.
As a hare's no hare when that hare is a witch,
no gras-bitere, no goibert, no lat-at-hom, no swikebert,
so Bolingbroke's heir is no heir to the throne,
the frend-lese, the wodecat, the brodlokere, the bromcat.
A hare-brained prince turned usurper king –
the purblinde, the fursecat, the louting, the westlokere.
The Rowston witch ran, as a hare in the night,
the waldenlie, the sidlokere, and eke the roulekere,
till a farmer brought it down in the dark, found it next day,
the stobhert, the lon-here, the strau-der, the lekere,
in human form – riddled with shot, not one for his pot
the wilde-der, the lerkere, the wint-swift, the skulkere.
Another village, and a cottage by the church – see there
the hare serd, the heg-roukere, the deudinge, the deu-hoppere,
see the hole in the wall, for a cat to come and go – or
the sittere, the gras-hoppere, the fitelfot, the fold-sittere.
And there's the Tetford witch, shape-shifting again –
the cawel-hert, the wortroppere, the go-bi-ground, the sittest-ille –

while the devil plays marbles in Dorrington church, or
the pitail, the toure-hohulle, the coue-arise, the make-agrise,
circles outside, March-haring widdershins under the moon,
the wit-wombe, the go-mit-lombe, the choumbe, the chauart.
No-one who meets him will ever fare well.

ST. OSWALD AND THE SHAFT OF LIGHT

Jane Simmons

A yuckker walked into The Poacher last night,
chrisom lookin' chap – bet he'd nivver done a day's work
in his life. By, he looked arrap an' well-moither'd –
like 'e'd bin dragged thro' an edge bakkerds,

a reet clapperdatch. An' 'e left door wide oppen!
Landlord shouts, "Are yer from Bardney?" –
but yucker din't shut door, just looked reet mazzled.
Nat from round 'ere, then – but one o' them frim folk.

Anyways, we called 'im ovver to warm up by the fire –
turns out 'e's one o' them high-falutin' university types,
Rory summat-or-other, writin' some big book abaht
Linkesheere folk-tales. 'E'd bin lookin' all ovver

fer Bardney Abbey, skellin' an scrammellin' abaht
ovver snaggy rocks an' stones till he near brained hissen.
Could we help him? For a pint, and a mention, of course…
Could we 'elp 'im? Of course we could – it'd be a pleasure!

We told 'im first abaht that there St Oswald –
'im as was brought to yon Abbey fer burial –

71

an' how the monks din't want his mowdy owd bones.
They only oppened wide the door an took 'im in

when they saw that shaft of bright holy light –
they were oppen all-hours to all-comers after,
which explains what landlord sez abaht the oppen door.
Then we towd him how sheep hereabouts is bred

Lopsided, to cope wi' our steep Linkesheere hills,
an' how them there rocks as stick up thro' yon fields
are teeth on our owd Bardney giant. An' blow me,
if daft bugger din't write it all down!

Some folk'll believe any owd kilter an' rammel!
After 'e'd closed his book and gone – shuttin' the door
after issen! – we was fit to burst, landlord included,
 whole pub-full on us, gawstering and hossacking.

How a'd love a bird's-eye view tomorrer, tho –
when same daft gump is diddle-daddlin' abaht
all day in high Linkesheere Wolds a-lookin fer
the famous Linkesheere Chalk Hare.

Author Comment

I chose subjects set in locations which feature in my family history. The poems, in their responses to existing narratives and uses of language, reflect my interest in challenging earlier narratives of women's lives, in myths, legends, and mediaeval texts.

'The Belvoir Witches' challenges the narrative told in the broadside ballad *The Damnable Practises of Three Lincolnshire Witches* (1619). It is informed by further details from contemporary documents and the memorial tablet for the then Earl and Countess of Rutland in Bottesford church.

'The Lincoln Imp' is based on a well-known story. In some versions, there is a second imp who escaped to Grimsby and continued to do mischief there, or continued to run round the outside of the cathedral – an explanation for windy conditions. I chose another version in which he is turned into stone and sits outside, high on the south wall. This linked his story to the peregrines which nest high on the cathedral, and offered an irresistible conclusion to the poem. The use of rhyming couplets and 'earthy' language seemed appropriate to this tale of mischief and comeuppance.

In 'Lincolnshire Hares', I wanted to write about the appearances of hares in local folklore – if I could find a way of linking them. Finally, I alternated my lines with ones from the anonymous thirteenth-century poem 'The Names of a Hare in English', a modern translation of which is in Seamus Heaney's 'The Names of the Hare'.

I had great fun writing 'St. Oswald and the Shaft of Light', which takes the story of the saint and his relics, and the origin of the saying 'Are you from Bardney', reframing both in a dialect version of a typical 'man walked into a bar' joke. In my version, the hapless researcher 'Rory summat-or-other' is easily duped into believing several tall tales before being sent on a wild goose chase.

MAIDENWELL

Robert Etty

When the stars and moon are bright
you might see from a grass path near Ostler's Lane
a white coach and horses dashing along.
The head of the coachman sits not on his neck

but on the seat by his bouncing backside
as he thrashes his translucent horses on.
Who's inside and where they're going is lost
with the road and few houses they pass.

The girl Cromwell's soldiers dropped down the well
they linked arms around so rope couldn't be thrown
left no pale imprint the future would doubt,
but a name on Lincolnshire's breath.

FARMER [BLANK] AND A HOBTHRUST

Robert Etty

Stories are told (and no doubt you've heard some),
in differing versions to various gatherings
in diverse places, of household familiars –
human-like, fairy-like, cats, rats, birds, ferrets –
who help and advise, guard and diagnose,
but often stray into malevolence.

A hobthrust selected East Halton, North Lincs,
as its residence, till it changed its mind:
an iron pot in a farmhouse cellar,
to be precise, and Mrs [Blank], who lived above,
described it (well, him) as "a little fellow
with a big head" and also "a kind of devil".

One account tells he only emerged
when the pot (full of children's thumb bones and sand)
was stirred slowly with a particular spoon,
and even then, not until twelve o'clock.
Happier, perhaps, is Version 8,
which states that he very soon bedded in –

so soon, in fact, that without being asked
he rounded up sheep for the shearing shed
and halved Farmer [Blank]'s workload overnight,
but once in a while he tired of good deeds
and turned his hand to mischief. One day
Farmer [Blank] found his cart on the roof

and a cartful of swedes rolling down the lane,
which sparked off a series of gentle pranks.
That year-end, instead of the fine linen shirt
the Hobthrust requested in payment for service,
disgruntled Farmer [Blank] laid a hemp shirt
by the hearth, and smirked, and plodded to bed.

hobthrusts aren't fools, and hemp isn't linen,
and howls of resentment and growls of anger
filled the dark house when he wriggled it on.
That itchy shirt ended a fine partnership
where the unwritten rules of give and take
bred a supernatural harmony.

Farmer and Mrs [Blank]'s farm fell in ruin,
and each unpaid labourer bade them goodbye.
They drove down the lane on their broken old cart,
and the word is they died in some big town or city.
This poem isn't sure where the hobthrust went next,
but Version 9 may take a shot at an answer.

SAINT PAULINUS AT FONABY TOP

Robert Etty

When Saint Paulinus was passing Caistor,
returning to York from a week in Skegness,
he met a farmer sowing corn.
Paulinus asked for some grain for his ass,
hoping that breakfast would sweeten its temper.

The farmer, not knowing of Saint Paulinus,
and not in the sweetest of moods himself,
replied, "[expletive]" and "[further expletive]"
and told a few lies about poor crops that year.
Then he grinned, "Anyroäd, 'ev a good trip!"

Spotting beside him a full sack of grain,
Paulinus pointed, "That's grain, in your sack."
"[Expletive]," the farmer replied. "Yon's a stoäne."
"In that case," Paulinus said, "stone shall it be,"
and solidified it with one hard stare.

The stone stood through winters and wars and plagues
until a new farmer, fond of relandscaping,
had it dragged home roped to twelve of his horses.
That afternoon, all twelve died, his son fell ill,
and his grain petrified. Seeing his folly,

he hitched up his last old horse, shouted "Pull!"
and watched, flabbergasted, the stone almost fly
up the hill to its same sunny field
and nestle in the warm soil and stubble,
putting its curse to bed (most of the time).

Hikers pass these days, but very few saints.
Those who have heard the tales tend not to pause,
while others rest there and gaze at the view,
as if the saint's ass had breakfasted,
and farmers and hikers lived trouble-free lives.

HAPPENINGS AT HALTON HOLEGATE

Robert Etty

Four walls keep many odd tales inside,
but brick floors are better at silencing them,
which brings to mind happenings at Halton Holegate.
Mrs Wilson, who didn't expect to,
played a lead role and, as it turned out,
might have laid a ghost as well as a floor.

Her odd tale's set in the windswept farmhouse
which she and Mr Wilson took over.
Tapping and knocking began one midnight
and swelled into furniture-dragging sounds
and crashes like pictures falling from hooks,
but dawn revealed that nothing had moved.

Their servant left for his sanity's sake,
but Mrs and Mr Wilson resolved
to give the knocks time to stop (which they did)
and concentrate on milking and calving
instead of checking the snecks and tiles.
That winter, while Mr Wilson snored,

Mrs Wilson had nursed a sick calf
when, wearily climbing the stairs to bed,
she saw, plain as day on the landing above,
a silently watching, round-shouldered old man.
He made a habit of guest appearances,
but here the story returns to brick floors.

The ridge underneath the sitting room carpet
had vexed Mrs Wilson for quite long enough,
and as she was prising up bricks to relay them
a stench rose and drifted from room to room
and put Mr Wilson off his boiled bacon.
He saved it for later, opened a window

and set about clearing the bricks and quicklime.
But his trowel snagged on something soft and flat,
so Mrs Wilson scraped with bare fingers
and teased out pieces of folded black silk,
inside one of which was a wedding ring.
And then she found bones, but not pig's or cow's.

Mrs Wilson was quizzed for the details
by journalists, gossips and clergymen.
The Illustrated Police News ran the story,
and several sensational publications
popularised it as far as New Zealand
before it lay down with the sitting room bricks.

Sitting rooms don't sit forever, of course,
and brick floors crumble when old houses fall,
but odd tales lodge at the backs of memories.
There's still talk of Mrs Wilson's sightings,
and sometimes a plough digs up broken red bricks.
Whole truths have been founded on less than this.

Author Comment

In preparation, I read a range of Lincolnshire folk tales in books and magazines and on several websites. There were some I had been aware of previously, but others were new to me. I seemed at first to be looking for familiar settings, but then events and characters in certain stories moved into focus, and combinations of factors led me to my selections.

A reader's letter in *Lincolnshire Life* in 1975 about Maidenwell's phantom coach intrigued me, and I have often remembered it when walking the footpaths or driving past road signs in that part of the Wolds. Similarly, knowing footpaths in the Caistor area drew me to the story of Saint Paulinus making his way across the same ground centuries ago. Sometimes when I notice an old farmhouse I wonder about the lives and times it might have witnessed, which may be why the stories involving farmhouses in East Halton and Halton Holegate particularly appealed to me.

A poem in draft does not necessarily know where it is heading. To an extent, their predetermined subjects made shaping these poems more straightforward, and I found that plots were falling into the kinds of lines and stanzas that I usually write. Then, as the stories developed inside the poems, spaces emerged for minor modifications and observations.

THE MARKBY CHURCH GHOST

Philippa East

2014

The sandwich triangles at the wake were small and dry – not what I'd pictured or what she would have wanted. But the catering had been a bit rushed and last-minute, the one part of her funeral plans Mum hadn't thought to prepare.

In the living room of Dad's old house, I set about peeling back the cling-film on the platters and encouraging people to come up and help themselves. I didn't take any of the sandwiches or quiche slices for myself. My appetite had shrivelled to almost nothing since I'd got the news.

"She lived a good life, you know," said a voice at my elbow.

I turned abruptly to find a man there, someone I vaguely recognised but couldn't entirely place. He stuck a hand out – the one that wasn't propping up a plate of egg sandwiches; he'd obviously got himself first in the queue. "Jack," he said. "One of Fiona's old school friends."

"Oh. Right." I hurried to return the handshake. He was tall, in his mid-fifties, black hair turning silver at his temples. "Thank you so much for coming." I looked down at his plate to avoid his face and the inevitable look of pity I'd find there.

There was a beat of silence, one of those ones I was getting used to, that sat there until someone filled it up with yet more trite phrases: *I'm sorry for your loss, how are you bearing up, at least she's at peace now…*

I wondered if this man knew I'd been in Australia when she died, on a delayed gap year, travelling, working odd jobs, trying to figure out what to do with my life. I hadn't even known she was ill. She had kept it to herself until it was too late. She'd been like that, my mum, Fiona McKendrick. Hard in odd ways. A rock. Probably she'd had to be, to do the job she did.

"Did you get enough to eat?" I said, to fill the gap.

"Yes, thank you, Molly."

He went silent again and my mind skittered off. She'd married – and had me – when she was barely twenty-one, twelve years younger than I was now, a crazy-young age it seemed to me. After she and my dad divorced, I'd stayed with my dad, here, in this house, until I went off to uni. Mum's job with the military had taken her all over and so it had been better for me – more stable – to stay with him. That was the simpler narrative, the one I mostly stuck with; better than examining the more tangled threads underneath. But either way, it meant that now there was so much I'd never had the chance to learn.

I smiled blandly at Jack, letting my eyes drift away over his shoulder. I was worn out from making small talk, not interested in Jack's inevitable platitudes, only in making my excuses and drifting away again.

"Did she ever tell you about the time we summoned a ghost?"

My head jerked in surprise. "What?"

Jack smiled. "She called me about it. This would have been" – he squinted, calculating – "a month or so before her diagnosis."

My head went a bit spinny. I wasn't following him. "When she was out in Afghanistan? She called you from there?"

"Yes." Jack nodded. "She wanted to ask what I remembered."

"Remembered about what?" He wasn't making any sense.

Jack took a bite of egg sandwich then cocked his head, recalling. "About the ghost. At Markby Church. This was all the way back in the '70s. But she still remembered after all that time."

1977

They were in the school library: her, Jack and Dougie, bored and restless as usual. All three of them had a Friday afternoon free period, but still with double maths to go before the end of the school week. Fiona was trying to read her assigned book for English – James Joyce's *A Portrait of the Artist as a Young Man* – but instead she'd got absorbed picking varnish off her fingernails. They weren't supposed to wear nail varnish, this being a Church of England school, but she'd slicked on a pale coral colour and miraculously so far none of the teachers had noticed.

"So… This weekend," said Dougie. "Want to, I dunno, get the bus into Boston?"

Jack shook his head. "Can't. No money." He was flicking through an old history book – no, not history. Fiona craned to look at the cover. Folk tales.

"You could come over to mine," she suggested. "Listen to some records." But they'd been to the music shop in Skegness last weekend, and there had been nothing new in the racks and they'd already listened to everything they owned a dozen times.

"I should probably stay in," said Dougie. "Catch up on homework."

Jack let out a scoffing laugh. "Yeah, right."

Dougie laughed too and stuck out his tongue. "It's so boring round here, though. Nothing to do. Soon as I'm old enough, I'm getting out. Moving to London."

Fiona leaned her cheek on her palm. "What are you reading, Jack? Lincolnshire legends? Don't tell me… The naughty imp and leaping Byard and Black Shuck the goblin dog."

"Yeah, yeah, all of those. Plus… this one." Jack turned the book round and held it up, pages splayed.

Dougie stopped swinging on his chair and leaned forward. "The Markby Church Legend. Wait – Markby? That's just up the road."

He was right. Fiona must have passed the low stone building loads of times, riding with her dad in the car.

"Go on then," said Dougie. "What does it say?"

Jack cleared his throat dramatically. "According to local legend, if you go to the church at midnight and run three times widdershins—"

"That means anti-clockwise," said Dougie.

Fiona rolled her eyes. "I know."

"—Run three times widdershins around it and bang a nail into the door, then—" Jack abruptly broke off and snapped the book closed.

"Then *what*, idiot?" said Dougie.

Jack growled in a throaty whisper. "You'll see a ghost."

Fiona sat back, shaking her head. "That's stupid." Even so, a small shiver ran up her spine. It wasn't that she *believed* in that stuff: ghost stories, folk tales, weird superstitions. It was just that she didn't like the idea of messing about with actual churches.

Jack bugged his eyes out at her. "Is it?"

She rolled her eyes again instead of answering, even as her stomach turned in slow circles.

Dougie pushed himself backwards to swing on his chair again, long legs dangling. "Fiona's right. It *is* stupid. Everyone knows that ghosts don't exist, and Lincolnshire's full of stupid folklore like that. Someone's even written a whole book about it. Still…"

Fiona looked at him. "What?"

"It's not like we've anything else to do this weekend."

2014

"So – what?" I said to Jack. "You went?"

He let out a soft laugh. "Like I said, we were just teenagers, mucking about."

"But you said *summoned* before. That you *summoned a ghost.*"

We'd stepped to one side of the living room now, leaving room for the rest of the guests to apply themselves to the buffet, and had landed up near the small side table where friends and relatives had laid out their favourite photographs of Mum, showing her in places and with people I'd never seen before. Dad would have loved these, but he'd died, too, six years ago. "But Mum didn't believe in that stuff, did she? She was an RAF Chaplain. She believed in God."

But even as I said the words, I felt strange, my limbs turning cold while little ripples of heat skated back and forth in my chest. I thought about the sense I'd had over the years that, at times, Mum had struggled horribly with her faith.

I folded my arms. "Anyway," I said "she definitely never told me about 'summoning a ghost.'"

"Okay, then," said Jack, smiling cautiously. "Shall I tell you now?"

1977

Fiona fingered the little brass nail in her dungarees pocket, dabbing its sharp tip against the pad of each finger. She was freezing, the wet grass soaking her platform boots, and her bum was numb too, sitting with Jack and Dougie on a toppled-over gravestone. About the only thing keeping the three of them warm was the dodgy cider Dougie had pilfered from home.

She took a fizzy sip and wiped her mouth. "Ugh. This stuff is rank."

"Keep drinking," said Dougie, "and you'll stop noticing in a bit."

"Ugh," Fiona repeated.

"Time check?" said Jack.

Dougie peered at the pale dial of his watch. "Eleven fifty-five."

A shiver ran through Fiona – and not just from the cold. "Are we really going to do this?" She had a strange feeling – like apprehension. Or a premonition. The air around them felt weighted and tense.

Dougie shrugged. "Why not? We're all here, aren't we?"

And Fiona had actually brought along a nail, the one a little crucifix used to hang from in her bedroom, until she got older and realised she should have Pink Floyd and Fleetwood Mac posters up on her walls instead.

Fiona took another, larger swig of cider before passing the bottle back to Dougie. She got up stiffly, denim flares damp. "Come on then. Let's get it over with."

At least there was a bright moon out, and stars. It was one of the things she liked most about Lincolnshire – the big, full skies. You could understand how people would literally walk about at night in the olden days. Once your eyes adjusted, it really was enough to see by.

Dougie screwed the top back onto the cider and squeezed the bottle into the pocket of his sheepskin coat. "So, do we start from the door then, or what?"

In the gloom, Jack shrugged. "The book didn't say, but – I guess?"

Fiona rolled her eyes, though it was probably too dark for them to see it. Together, they made their way towards the squat, thatched church – the only thatched church in Lincolnshire, apparently! Once they got up close, Fiona made out strange speckles all over the door. She turned to the boys. "Look." The thick wood was pitted with little holes. Hands a bit shaky, she ran her fingers over them. There were nail heads buried in the door, too – dozens and dozens of them.

"Wow. Okay," said Dougie, "so… it's true, then?"

Jack let out a tight laugh. "It's true other people have *tried* it."

Fiona felt another wave of apprehension sweep through her. Until now, it had been a joke, a game. Nothing more than silly words in a dumb book. But now, being here, seeing all these other nails…

The clang of a distant church bell made them jump. Fiona pressed a hand to her chest. Her heart was racing. The three of them stared at each other in the gloom as the bells chimed *ten… eleven… twelve…* Before she could open her mouth to say, *um, guys are we sure about this…?* Jack gave a whoop and was off, charging away to the right – running widdershins.

Dougie let out an answering yelp. Before she could do anything, he grabbed Fiona's arm, yelling "Come on!"

And then she was stumbling, tripping on the uneven ground in her clumsy platforms, dizzy from the cider that was suddenly hitting. She steadied herself on the stone wall, grazing her palm as she stumbled round the first corner. She could hear Dougie and Jack's feet crashing on the flagstones up ahead and the rasp of her panting breath.

"Slow down," she shouted as they made it once round. "Wait for me!" She sounded like a whiny child. She kept running.

Twice round. Her breath stung her chest. This was stupid. Really so stupid, but she was already two and a half times round now, and she found her hand involuntarily slipping into her dungarees pocket, grasping the nail there, its sharp point ready.

At the door, Jack and Dougie were muttering breathlessly. "Hang on – use a stone! Look, here, bang it with this" – because none of them had thought to bring any kind of hammer.

She caught them up just in time to watch Jack pound in his steel nail. He was laughing, fumbling the random chunk of rock he'd picked up, *bang, bang, bang*, and suddenly Fiona realised how much it sounded like knocking.

Bang, bang, bang. Now Dougie was hammering in his own nail, too.

"Your turn!" Dougie was holding out the rock to her, grinning like a maniac in the moonlight. All of them, she realised, had drunk way too much cider.

As though in a dream, she took the stone.

Her tiny brass nail was so slim and fine that she barely needed to tap it. *Tap, tap, tap*, such a gentle knocking, but the nail slid right in, almost as though being drawn through from inside.

Legs shaking, she stepped back. "Now what?" she whispered.

A gust of wind rustled the thatch of the roof, seeming to echo her question.

2014

I stared at Jack. "Well?" I said, impatiently. "What did you see?"

Jack set his empty plate aside and laughed. "Nothing."

"Nothing? But you said…"

He cocked his head again.

I huffed out a sigh. He was milking this, but on the other hand, I didn't really mind. I was glad of something to take my mind off everything, and this conversation was preferable to the typical stilted exchanges I'd had these last two weeks, even if it was a morbid tale about churches and summoning spirits – and my mum.

"So you banged your nails in, and then what?"

"Well, at first we stood around for, like, fifteen minutes, freezing our bums off. And then…"

"Then…?"

"Your mum had… I guess these days you'd call it a panic attack."

"A panic attack?"

"We were back on the road home, finally leaving, when she looked back. Then she freaked out. Claimed she saw something."

I sized him up sceptically, trying to read his expression. "A ghost?" I said dryly.

Jack spread his hands out. "What else?"

I gave a wry smile. Maybe they never even went to Markby Church. Maybe this whole story was made up. But I didn't mind playing along. I liked Jack, and at least he was keeping me entertained, staving off the black sadness I knew would wrap round me that night.

"So," I said, "what did this 'ghost' look like?"

Something flickered over Jack's face, a more serious expression, and for a moment I thought perhaps he wasn't spinning tales after all.

"Fiona – your mum – said she saw a figure. Male or female, she wasn't sure. Wearing blurry beige. With a purple scarf."

I wrinkled my nose. What kind of apparition was that? "A beige ghost. In a purple scarf?" This tale had really fallen apart at the climax.

"That's what she said. And she stuck to that story. Even decades later."

"Yes." I hesitated. "The phone call from Afghanistan you mentioned."

"That's right. She wanted to know what I remembered."

"About a beige figure in a purple scarf?"

Jack smiled at me. "Yes."

I thought about it, processing, trying to make sense of the mystery. Despite myself, the hairs on my neck were standing up. "What about your friend Dougie? What does he remember?"

Jack gave a regretful shrug. "I don't know, we lost touch. He moved to London." He smiled. "Went his own way, like he said he would."

"The funny part," he went on, "is that Fiona began her religious studies soon after that night. Switched her A-levels. You know, even at school, unlike the rest of us, she always had... a kind of faith."

"She did? That early?"

"You didn't know that?"

I shook my head and swallowed. "No. There was a lot I didn't know about my mum. But you know – what you're saying, it makes a kind of sense. I always suspected something drove her to study theology, become a chaplain. Something that had happened. And also that... deep down, she always struggled with her faith."

Jack looked at me, his deep eyes meeting mine. "You're right. I really think that she did."

2013

Instinctively, Fiona ducked at the thunder of a chopper. She thought she'd be used to the noises by now, but she wasn't. Not at all. As she wasn't even stationed anywhere near the front lines, just at Camp Bastion. Far from home, but hardly in any danger. So why did she feel so fragile all the time?

In the tent she shared with two other chaplains, she sat hunkered on her camp bed, pressing to her lips the crucifix that hung round her neck. She closed her eyes, listening for the voice – the one that had fallen silent this last... how long was it now? Weeks? Months?

So long.

She tried to calm herself and create that place of open stillness in her mind. But there was only nothingness. A blank. An abject absence of belief in herself or her purpose.

She shook her head and pressed her palms to her eye sockets. Why now, of all times? Why now, when she needed to be at her absolute best? She'd experienced these lapses in faith all her life. They came on like waves of depression, except that they didn't just bring sadness or fatigue or lack of motivation.

They brought shameful doubt, questioning the path she had chosen. Not believing herself worthy. They brought a terrifying silence in her heart.

Muscles aching, she got up from her bed and made her way to the cookhouse, as though she could fill the emptiness with chocolate brownies and soup.

She clattered an empty plate onto a tray and joined the queue of her colleagues, a line of pale brown DPM fatigues. Mac and cheese. With chips. As she took a seat at one of the long tables, she tried to ground herself. She was an RAF Padre, administering to those who served Queen and country. And through that, serving God.

Yet still, when she closed her eyes at night, the figure came to her: cloudy, blurred. She could never get a glimpse of its face. It didn't do anything, didn't say anything. Just stood there and looked at her.

The Markby Church ghost.

Fiona jumped as someone set their own tray down next to hers with a clatter.

"Excuse me, Padre. Mind if I join you?"

She shook her head and made space; it was Lieutenant Colonel Merritt, one of the army surgeons. She swallowed a sharp chip and made herself speak. "How is he?"

She didn't need to spell out who she was talking about: the young man who lay right now in the camp's field hospital, with internal bleeding and one whole leg blown off.

Merritt shook his head. He looked terrible. "Not good. Not good at all."

Fiona felt sick.

"That's why I came to find you. We're going to need you, any hour now. He's a religious man. He's asked for last rites."

Fiona felt herself grow numb inside. She had been required for this only twice before in her career. Both times her faith had been strong and high, and even then it had taken almost every ounce of her spiritual strength. How was she supposed to manage now, when she had nothing but emptiness inside?

Almost before she could stop herself, the words slipped out: "I don't think—"

Merritt turned to her in confusion, and she managed to clamp her teeth on the rest just in time.

"Absolutely," she said instead. "I'll come right away."

2014

"I still don't get it," I said, as Jack helped me gather up the discarded plates for the dishwasher. Most of the mourners had left now, slipping away back to their ordinary lives. My palm felt raw from being grasped and shaken, my shoulder bruised from all the solicitous patting. Jack was still here, though. We were still talking. "Why did she call you then?"

"I don't know. Like I said, she wanted to know what we saw that night."

"You mean what *she* saw. You said you and Dougie didn't see anything."

"Yes. Right. All I could do was repeat back what I remembered her telling me. But…"

"But what?"

"That seemed to… I don't know. Bring her relief."

"Relief?" I rubbed my forehead trying to make sense of this, then before I could stop them, tears escaped from my eyes – the first tears I'd cried in weeks.

"I'm so sorry, Molly! I never meant to upset you."

I shook my head. "You haven't. You didn't." Angrily, I wiped the tears away. "It's just… I was on the other side of the world when she died, because she didn't tell me – or she did but not properly – but I should have realised how serious things were. I should have known Mum would put a brave face on things. She went through all the tests and treatments alone, and – and then when it all took such a sharp downturn at the end, I wasn't able to get back in time."

My nose was running now. Clumsy with frustration, I hunted in my jeans pocket for a tissue, but there were only shreds of an old one in there. Suddenly I wanted to scream at the world, for all the unfairness and everything that had gone wrong.

"Here." Jack was holding out a clean, folded paper napkin. I took it from him and noisily blew my nose.

"I'm sorry," I said. "I didn't mean to go off like that. It's just – I wasn't there. I want to believe she was okay at the end. Her faith… it was so important to her. But I wasn't there, so I don't know, and I'm torn up by the thought that she wasn't at peace when she died."

Jack nodded, understanding. "All I can tell you is that, in that phone call, she seemed okay. Really okay. Like something profound had shifted."

I shook my head. "But what? How? Because of some silly hallucination she had as a schoolgirl?"

Jack shook his head. "I don't know, Molly."

That night, when the house was silent again and everyone had gone home, I curled up in my bed – the bed I'd slept in all through childhood, before I went off roaming the world – hugging my knees to my chest and thinking.

After an hour, I knew there was no way I was going to get any sleep, so I got up, padded down to the cold kitchen and opened my laptop. In the search bar, I typed: *the Markby Church Ghost*.

It wasn't hard to find details of the folk tale, and what I found wasn't much more than what Jack had already said. You ran three times round the church anti-clockwise, then banged a nail into the door. Do it at midnight, and a ghost would appear.

Mum had done it as a teenager, apparently. And apparently she had seen something – something that had haunted her ever since.

I read through all the Markby Ghost stories I could find, but none of them shed any kind of light. People claimed to have seen monks, skeletons, headless horsemen, all sorts. But you couldn't believe the crap you read online.

And it was so silly anyway what Jack had described: a blurry beige figure in a purple scarf. How could that have brought my mum any solace? At the time, it had only brought on a panic attack.

Except –

A shock ran through me.

Unless –

I scraped back my chair and stumbled to my feet, banging my shin on the table leg as I hurried through to the living room, to the side-table where friends and loved ones had left me their favourite photos of Mum.

I clicked on a lamp, scrabbling through them, skin shivering. There were pictures of her with her parents, with university friends, with me as a baby, at her military graduation, her fortieth birthday bash…

And here. My hands shook as I lifted it up to the light.

I stumbled to the sofa, emotions washing through me like a tidal wave. I stared at the photo, wanting to laugh out loud at the way it suddenly all made sense. What she had seen that night. What she must have realised.

2013

Fiona got to her feet, her lunch barely touched, and followed Lt. Col. Merritt along the walkway towards the camp's field hospital. They were almost there when she stopped short.

"Wait – I'm sorry," she said, "I need to fetch something. Give me two minutes and I'll be right along."

He nodded, and she hurried back to her tent. Out here, there was little pomp or ceremony, not like back home when preaching a full service in a church. But there was still one thing she needed for this task.

She ducked down to the footlocker at the end of her bed. Inside, the embroidered sash sat neatly folded on its shelf. She ran her fingers over the intricate stitching, its finery incongruous against the messy beige and brown of her fatigues. Legs hollow, she lifted it out and carefully placed the purple stole around her neck, letting it hang down from either shoulder. She stood in front of the scratched vertical mirror that was propped against the far wall and looked at herself.

Stared.

Stared again.

Hands shaking, she fumbled in her pocket for her phone card, picturing the camp's pay phones, dragging from her memory the number she would call.

2014

That night, I slept with the photo of Mum tucked under my pillow. When I woke in the bright light of the morning, I saw the words written lightly on the back:

From Jack.

Author Comment

Having lived in Lincolnshire for the last ten years, I was delighted to get involved in this fascinating project. I hopped on the project website, lincolnshirefolktalesproject.com, and quickly found myself immersed in all the folk tales on there, amazed by the depth and wealth of stories surrounding me, my creative mind whirring…

I'm a psychological thriller writer by background, so these tales of suspicion, mystery and peril were right up my street! I've also always been drawn to the eerie and paranormal, so having the chance to write my own ghostly tale felt like a wonderful opportunity.

As I scanned through the various stories, I found myself drawn time and again to the tale of the Markby Church Ghost – especially the detail of the myriad tiny holes and nail heads in the church door, showing just how many people have tried to summon this infamous apparition over the decades. Right away, I found myself wondering who in the modern era would choose to test out such an uncanny ritual – and at once there came to mind a group of bored and restless Lincolnshire teenagers. This was probably because my latest psychological thriller, A Guilty Secret, features a similar cast of troubled teens, who perform their own spooky games in the woods behind their exclusive Scottish boarding school.

I originally moved to Lincolnshire when my spouse (a doctor with the RAF) was posted to Cranwell in 2013. My experiences in Lincolnshire are therefore closely bound up with the county's long connections with the RAF, and this became another key narrative thread in my modernised folk tale.

I do hope readers of my tale will enjoy it as much as I enjoyed writing it, and I am proud to add my own small slice of storytelling to this wonderful Lincolnshire Folk Tales anthology.

21:00 – 22:00, TIDDY MUN. NEW SERIES. (S) (HD)

Fee Griffin

To be a fen dweller without a name, no
horse (no name) no

>>> hills, no name
>>> no house;

to be

> a fertility spirit but more concerned with the water level
> feels like a Channel 4 documentary:

Davina or Dawn
maybe Anna   pours a pail of water
                    into flat country
                    at midnight,
                    says to camera:

>>> *I know you think you know what flat
>>> looks like, but get a load of thissss!*

[cut away to the lighting director, weeping]
[cut away to a bog at midnight]

No, not flat like a hand-drawn horizon,
flat like a bulldozed king –
the first ruler

/taciturn field line
/in real time

[captured with Steadicam]

The gameshow contestants, interviewed later in life, will reject
any suggestion that the show had a detrimental effect,

even if/
even if/
even if/   their future boss saw them naked;
even if/   there was record rainfall, or livestock put at risk;
even if/   their colleague walks in as they become level
             with the field like an unprecedented volume of
             water −

To be surrounded by flooding salt flats, but more concerned
with Dutch drainage expertise of the seventeenth century,
feels like a second Channel 4 documentary:

Davina, Dawn or Anna stand near a drainage ditch
                    This water's thruff!
                    [wink to camera]

Now, each member of a team of friends prepares a bucket
with a micro-camera and a tracking device

feels like/
feels like/
             feels more like *The Crystal Maze*

O, they are excited! They have matching leisure
wear – a little retro – they are estate agents they
are account managers and train engineers they
are Elaine & Steve & Helen

Elaine & Steve & Helen have been positioned
(by the production assistants)

in mud/sandflats/saltmarsh and dunes
Tell us a bit about yourself!

I love the water near a cross dyke,
declares Elaine, and there is functional
applause off/
       stage left.
The remaining contestants
smile warmly. Steve is wearing a T-shirt that reads

I♥ flat, dry, low-lying
agricultural regions

and Helen just continues to sink until assorted Dutch
masters build dykes higher and higher to protect her from
flooding. You're thinking Rembrandt and Van Gogh; the
production crew is thinking Cornelius Vermuyden.
Allegories, man! The earth walls come to Helen's knees; her
shins are a foot or so below sea level and

even though the path is open to them all
to accumulate peat
in an old tuxedo
and bow out

for the evening
no-one does.

The production designers worry they are not producing an
iconic enough still frame for the ad break card, when –

[nieuwe maan!]
[Tha pownies get lame; the lambs dwindle]
[tha creed meal brunt 'issen an' tha new milk curdles]

[tha thatch falls in, an' tha walls burst out
an' all an' anders went arsy-varsy]

Tiddy Mun? *Tiddy Mun?*
Someone points a camera.

Players!
Gather near a drainage ditch [white heed, walkin' lame]
[While tha watter teems tha fen
Tiddy Mun'll hurt nane]

Each player brings a pail of water to the studio, to prove to
Davina or Dawn or Anna or the production crew or Tiddy
Mun that they're not responsible for the drainage of the
Carrs. [meanwhile, seventeenth century, Cornelius
Vermuyden winks off-stage left]

Davina or Dawn or Anna winks back
[post-production adds a twinkle decal]

Nothing wrong with a nice full thruff!
[Side eye from Davina/Dawn/Anna]

Years later, the contestants are interviewed on the subject by a national newspaper. Much depends on the narrator.

My mum's 83; she knew I went on the fens, but she didn't watch it, says Steve (not his real name). He applied to be 'villager #3 (carr folk)' shortly after the end of a tough relationship. *I was having a bit of a midlife crisis. I was in my 40s then, so I was like: do you know what? I want to do something way out there.*

[Tiddy Mun appears left, holding a boom pole]
[Tiddy Mun does not appear]

What kind of person tips a pail of water at midnight? asks Helen, 50, from Essex, who has since appeared on the fen twice.

[Tiddy Mun marries the ancient right to cut turf at first sight]
[Tiddy Mun is sponsored by naane]

They pour their pails and the watter rises,
low lying, highfalutin watter watter watter

There is great excitement in the team of friends!

The production assistant moves to reposition Tiddy Mun due to a camera angle change and for the next 12 months wakes nightly with water in her ears.

> *I had to empty glasses of water in front of these two complete strangers, and talk about water spirits and low-lying countries like the Netherlands and Bangladesh,* explains Elaine. *It was just this little office room with the blinds down.*

By morning, the waters would subside and the problem
return.During the ad break, the contestants and the editing
team set about   cutting/
              cutting/
         cutting/
         turf, or peat, an ancient right, a turbary, for fuel
on a particular area of bog meanwhile watte/r
wat/ter w/atter watter // cutting in like Biff in the
Enchantment Under the S— no no not under the sea.
Keep it together.
               Keep it together, Helen.

Angered by these events which affected the pools in which
he lived, and voted off after revealing his face –
           [Tiddy Mun does not appear]

– he dries out this
poem right in front
of you
           [Tha pownies get lame; the lambs dwindle
                              etc]

Did you have so many crows feet before?
cut/
     cut/
     cut/

Players! Gather near a drainage ditch [white heed, walkin'
lame]
           [While tha watter teems tha fen
           Tiddy Mun'll hurt nane]

You fall asleep watching *Saving Lives at Sea*, awake
at midnight to discover you have saved 0 lives at sea.
The sky is dark

[nieuwe maan]

Elaine, Steve and Helen are depending on you!
The production assistant hands you

an alarm clock,
a pail of water, and
stands back—

MMXXIV

Author Comment

I am struck by how relevant the old tale of Tiddy Mun is to the unfolding environmental catastrophes of our times. I wanted to connect the two for the reader, to bring some of Tiddy Mun into their ordinary lives.

If my poem does not seem like a complete (or even *partially* complete) rendition, this is deliberate. As Matthew Zapruder notes, 'poetry can only be fully pursued when the writer is not ultimately preoccupied with any other task, like storytelling or explaining or convincing or describing or anything else.' In other words, it is important that the poem, first and foremost, should be allowed to move and function as a poem, in its act of what Zapruder calls 'associative daydreaming'. If the reader is inspired to learn more about the myth, that is their choice. I decided to frame this within a familiar context: reality television. By using 'found text' which drew on a range of academic papers and media stories, I hope the reader gets a sense of the complexity of the Tiddy Mun myth and may feel connected to it by one or more of these approaches.

While Tiddy Mun was never completely benign (folklorist Ethel Rudkin notes that, even in good times, he caused locals to feel "shivery-like"), it is only with the seventeenth-century draining of the Carrs and Fens that he appears to have become a frightening figure. The accompanying rise in illness (the fen drainage 'may […] have contributed to an increase in mosquito- and fly-borne illnesses', as Darwin Horn notes) are attributed to his anger. Relations with the Tiddy Mun took on a more ecological bent at this time, as people attempted to appease him with assurances they were not responsible for the destruction of his environment, tipping a pail of water into the cross dyke on a new moon with the words "Tiddy Mun, wi'out a name/ here's watter for thee, tak th' spell undone!" This sensitivity to the environment and its effects on health, wellbeing and livelihood are playing out again today, just as surely as reality TV keeps on rolling.

LAST RITES
OR A TALE OF TOM OTTER
Anne Zouroudi

Lincolnshire, 1860

To Thomas Miller, this land – unendingly flat, broken up by unkempt hedges and broad ditches – is alien and tedious. On and on the empty fields go by, sodden under the weight of November's rain, stretching away to a bleak horizon where at last they meet the drab, grey sky.

Coming from a pretty village in the undulating Wolds, to Miller's eye this landscape holds a paucity of interest: from time to time a stand of windswept elms with rooks crying overhead, or some lonely roadside house where unfriendly dogs bark at the gate.

A glance at his pocket watch shows another hour at least before they reach Lincoln. At only just past two, the light's already fading, as if the day has surrendered all hope of the weather's improvement. Leaning through the carriage window, he shouts to the driver to push on faster, though he knows his demand is unreasonable. The turnpike is claggy, the horses exhausted.

Removing his hat, he wraps his blanket tighter round his knees, closes his eyes and tries to sleep.

He must have dozed, since the slowing of the horses wakes him.

A man has joined him inside the carriage.

Miller is startled. The carriage is a private hire, an indulgence following a recent professional success, and the man is trespassing on his comfortable solitude. His face is hidden by a wide-brimmed felt hat pulled down over his eyes, but Miller takes him for a youngish fellow of twenty-three or four, broadly built and strong. His labourer's coat and trousers are dirty, and his boots so heavy with mud he must have walked some distance along the turnpike.

Under such cold and wet conditions, Miller tells himself he would not normally object to giving a working man the benefit of a mile or two in the carriage's relative comfort; but a dank and frankly putrid odour is coming off the fellow's clothing, which Miller cannot help but find objectionable.

The horses have slowed to a stop.

One of the coachmen has jumped down from his seat, and presents himself outside Miller's window.

"Saxilby toll, Sir," he says. "We'll take a few minutes to let the horses catch their breath, and we'll be on our way again."

Miller wants to quiz him about his unwanted companion, but unable to think of any way to do so without appearing boorishly rude, he resolves instead to take up the matter when they arrive at their destination. In any case, the coachman has already gone away to find water for the animals.

Deciding to make the best of it, Miller turns to ask his fellow traveller if he's familiar with the road and how much longer it will take to reach the city.

Though surprised, he's pleased to see the young man is gone; though the offensive smell he brought with him remains stubbornly behind.

As the afternoon draws to its close, Miller is relieved to reach the Saracen's Head inn on Lincoln's High Street. A room is prepared for him, though he finds it bitterly cold, and the fire smouldering in the grate – more smoke than flame – appears unlikely to raise the temperature. After supper, a pleasant girl who gives her name as Hannah brings him a hot water bottle. The room is gloomy, and he asks her for another lamp since he wishes to read. She tells him she will bring candles when she next comes upstairs, but time goes by and she doesn't return.

So, more for the warmth of the blankets than out of fatigue, Miller puts himself to bed.

The lamp burns low and the inn falls quiet, though the night-time noises sound loud: the scuttling of mice behind the panelled walls, the patter of rain against the window, the creak of a floorboard by his door as someone walks along the passage outside.

The lamp goes out.

With the velvet curtains drawn and not even a glow left in the fire, the darkness is complete. Miller feels a frisson of anxiety, an echo of boyhood terrors when his fear of the dark was assuaged only by leaving his own bed and crawling in to sleep with his brother. Outside his door, the floorboard creaks again, and for no good reason an image comes to his mind of the young man who joined him in his carriage this afternoon past, standing silent outside the closed bedroom door.

In the morning, he draws back the curtains on the feeble light of another raw winter's morning.

Shivering, he takes a poker to the ashes in the grate, then finds a few pieces of bark in the log basket, places them in the dead heart of the fire and blows to raise a flame. His effort is in vain; but being so close to the fire surround, he notices a number of criss-crossed lines crudely cut into the wood, making a lattice-like pattern.

Hannah bustles in, placing a jug of hot water for his ablutions on the dresser.

"There's a real chill in here, isn't there?" she says. "Usually this room's warm as toast. Mind you, it's a cold enough morning outside, fog so thick you can't see your hand in front of your face."

"May I ask," he says, "what are these marks on the fireplace?"

He points out the carved lattice, and her face becomes solemn. "That's a charm against witches and demons."

"In a civilised place such as this?"

Hannah seems in earnest. "You've never heard of the Lincolnshire witches? You have to be careful, they like to come in down the chimney. Don't look so worried, that mark there will keep them out. They see that and they can't go past it. Anyway, cook says to tell you breakfast is laid downstairs."

Miller finds the dining room empty of other guests. The landlord – a stooping, dismal man whose ruddy nose suggests an affection for drink – serves him cold ham, sharp cheese, and bread baked to almost inedible hardness.

"Shall you be eating luncheon with us, Sir?" the landlord asks, placing a pot of mustard next to the pickles. "They're wanting to know in the kitchen."

"I shall," says Miller. "Please set the table for two. I'm expecting a business associate to join me, Mr Edward Cousans. When he arrives, you'll find me in the reading room."

"Very good," says the landlord, "I'll tell Hannah to bank up the fire."

The reading room is made pleasant by an arrangement of comfortable chairs, a shelf of passably readable books and an excellent selection of the more popular newspapers and journals.

Miller takes the latest edition of the *Lincoln Chronicle* to a seat between the fire and a window, where he can both be warm and have sufficient light to read. The Italianate clock on the mantelpiece chimes the half hour. With some time to wait before his guest arrives, Miller opens the newspaper.

Yet as he turns to page two, the landlord appears in the doorway.

"'Scuse me, Sir, but your guest is here."

"Really?" Miller glances at the clock, which has not yet struck the three-quarter hour. "Well, he's damned early. Send him in, then, send him in."

Miller stands and straightens his cravat, ready to greet his friend.

But the man who enters is a stranger of around thirty, dressed in the cheap coat and breeches of a clerk – though the clothes are a tight fit, as if borrowed from someone not his size, while razor-nicks on his chin and an uneven hairline suggest recent and hasty barbering. He's holding a small wooden chest, rustic in appearance, the lid secured with a worn piece of blue ribbon, which he places on the table where the journals are displayed, as if glad to be relieved of its weight.

The stranger holds out his hand to be shaken. "Please, forgive my intrusion, Mr Miller. Walter Rawlinson, at your service."

"You have the advantage of me," says Miller, irked at being disturbed. "I don't believe we've been introduced."

"We haven't," concedes Rawlinson, lowering his unshaken hand. "But might I beg a few minutes of your time? I've information I believe you'll find of interest, and which might even be to your benefit financially."

The suggestion of a monetary advantage persuades Miller to agree. Pointing Rawlinson to a chair, he retakes his own.

"May I ask how you know who I am?"

"I have a relative employed in the hotel," says Rawlinson. "She recognised your name, and told me you were here. People locally regard you as a celebrity. I want to speak to you concerning a story you had published last year."

"Namely?"

"The tale of Tom Otter."

Miller takes pride in the story, some of his best work. "In the *Lincoln Chronicle*, yes. Obviously you've read it."

"Oh yes, I've read it many times through. I've pored over the details, and much admired the quality of your writing."

Miller bows his head modestly.

"The only problem I see with it," Rawlinson goes on, "is that factually, it's almost entirely incorrect."

Untroubled, Miller smiles. "Well, Mr Rawlinson, I'm sure you're not naïve enough to believe that everything you see in print is entirely truthful. Newspapers must first and foremost appeal to their readers, and so are in the business of entertainment. The history of Tom Otter provided the base for a novel and engaging story, which as you suggest has sold particularly well."

"But people have been hurt by your untruths, Mr Miller. My own family, most of all."

"What has your family to do with Tom Otter?"

"He was my grandfather."

Face-to-face with a relation of someone he's maligned, Miller is discomfited. "Then I should apologise. But Otter was convicted of a particularly vicious murder. Does that not make him fair game?"

"I don't think so." Rawlinson sits forward in his chair. "I'm here to make you a proposal, so let me begin by establishing my *bona fides*. My grandmother was Martha Rawlinson, Tom's first and only legal wife. Any information I offer you I have directly from her, or via my mother from my paternal great-grandfather and Tom's father Robert, who visited Tom in Lincoln jail several times. By all accounts Robert was a dour and reticent man, but he spoke passionately about Tom, who was the favourite of his children and the apple of his eye. When Tom was hanged, Robert performed the only last service to his son that was permitted him: to hang onto Tom's legs as he dangled from the rope, thus breaking his neck and ending his suffering. You will agree I'm sure that no parent should ever be forced to perform such a drastic act. Worse, though, was in store for him. The horror of seeing the crowds mock his son's corpse as he dangled in the gibbet all but turned Robert's mind."

Miller adopts a sympathetic expression, though inwardly he's cursing himself for an opportunity missed: a grief-stricken father rushing to hasten his son's death on the gallows is a sensational detail he might have included to great benefit in his fabricated history of Otter's end.

"As for my grandmother, she and Tom married at Christmas of 1804. My mother Maria was born shortly after, in all honesty with only days to spare to make her legitimate. There was no love in the marriage – my grandmother was honest about that – but she spoke fondly of my grandfather, and often said how handsome he was."

"Many a handsome face hides a black soul," says Miller.

"You do him wrong," counters Rawlinson. "The story as you have written it makes no sense. My grandfather was not guilty of the crime for which he was so cruelly punished."

Miller bristles. "In what way, no sense? I based my account on respectable newspaper reports of the time."

"One journalist embroidering the invented words of others, perhaps? Please, consider the facts. Mary Kirkham's family were from North Hykeham, only a mile away from here, and they live there still. My grandfather was renting a room behind the Pack Horse inn just along the street, where – you'll remember from your article – the constables arrested him for murder. He and Mary were married in the church of St Mary Wigford, just a few steps away. How far do you suppose the church is from the spot where Mary's body was found?"

Miller considers. As he recalls, Otter's victim was found at Drinsey Nook, close to the Saxilby toll where his coach halted yesterday. After that, almost another two hours passed before they reached the Saracen's Head, but the conditions were poor and a further stop was made for a change of horses when one of the beasts went lame.

"I'd hesitate to guess," he says.

"Let me then tell you. I estimate the journey to be around seven miles, possibly eight. A substantial distance on foot in the depths of winter, wouldn't you say?"

"Quite substantial, yes."

"And if you were a lady eight months pregnant, you'd make very slow progress, don't you agree?"

"I should say so."

"So what might persuade a woman in her condition to leave her home and family, and attempt such a gruelling journey?"

"I really couldn't say."

"Then may I suggest an answer? Shall I tell you what Tom told his father whilst he was locked away in Lincoln jail?"

"Please do."

"Tom described Mary as a lady of the night. That he had relations with her, he never denied, but as to being the father of her child, he reckoned his chances to be no better than one in a hundred. He believed Mary named him to the constables as he was young and a hard worker, while the biggest part of her clients were drunks or elderly and themselves only a short step away from begging parish assistance.

"According to Robert, when the constables arrived to force Tom into marriage with Mary, he saw no point in objecting. His existing wife – my grandmother – was still living at Hockerton where they were wed, and couldn't be produced. Realising no one could prove if he were married or not, for Mary's sake he went through the ceremony giving my grandmother's maiden name of Temporel, thinking no one would be any the wiser."

"He was casual, then, about his bigamy," says Miller. "Hardly an upstanding character."

"I agree. But by Tom's account, Mary was afraid to give birth at the family home. Her father and brother had recently been plagued by sickness Mary believed was typhoid. So Tom suggested that for her lying-in she might go to his family's farm at Treswell in Nottinghamshire. He was certain that if Robert believed her baby was of Otter blood, he would offer Mary a Christian welcome and see she was cared for. I wonder if you consulted a map when you were writing your sensationalist story, Mr Miller?"

"I saw no reason to be poring over maps. Why would I?"

"Because a map would have shown you that Tom's statement of Mary's destination was very likely true. You could almost draw a straight line between the church of St Mary Wigford and the village of Tresswell, with a ferry to cross the River Trent at Torksey in between. That is what my grandfather said at his trial."

"With no bearing on his guilt. The couple walked a great distance, the woman was tired and complaining, he did away with her."

"Ah, but it does have a bearing. If that part of his account was plausible, why should the rest not be so? I have done more calculations. The day of their wedding – the third of November 1805 – was a Sunday, my grandfather's one free day of the week. As he told it to his father – and the court which tried him – he'd had a recent promotion to foreman, and was very unwilling to miss work on Monday morning and risk losing his new post. So he sent ahead a message to an acquaintance of his in Saxilby, one John Dunberley. He and Dunberley had worked together in that area, and shared lodgings. Tom asked Dunberley to meet him on the turnpike near the village, saying he'd pay him to escort Mary the remainder of the way to his father's farm."

There are voices in the hall outside. The door of the reading-room opens, and the landlord shows in a gaunt-featured man, who as he enters hands his astrakhan-collared overcoat to the landlord, along with his fashionable Bowler hat.

"There you are, Thomas," he says to Miller. "Ah, forgive me, you're engaged. I'll wait for you in the dining room."

"No, no, stay," says Miller. "Landlord, let's have a glass of wine here, a claret if you have one."

As the landlord leaves, Miller addresses Rawlinson. "This is Mr Edward Cousans, proprietor and editor of the *Lincoln Chronicle*. Edward, this young gentleman is Walter Rawlinson, and he's taking me to task over my treatment of his relative in your newspaper. He claims to be none other than the grandson of Tom Otter."

"Does he, by God?" Cousans takes a chair close to the fire. "To be related to such a ruffian is nothing to boast of, surely? If I were you, Sir, I'd be keeping such a connection to myself."

"Mr Rawlinson was just imparting to me his theory of his grandfather's innocence," says Miller. "So far, I've heard nothing to persuade me."

"Then let him try and convince me." Cousans steeples his fingertips and holds them to his thin, pale lips, while Rawlinson summarises what he's said.

"And did Otter and this fellow Dunberley keep their appointment?" asks Cousans, when Rawlinson's done.

"My grandfather claimed they did," says Rawlinson, "and that he gave Dunberley money, and Mary too. Dunberley was to take Mary to an inn to spend the night, and continue with her the following day, while my grandfather set off on foot back to Lincoln.

"Then the following morning, Dunberley, all agitated, raised the alarm, stating that he'd stumbled across Mary's body. Her head and face were so battered you'd think she'd be impossible to identify, given she was a stranger in that place. Yet someone named her. Who else, except Dunberley? And who put forward the name of Tom Otter as her assailant if not him? Who were the twenty witnesses at his trial who swore they recognised him on the road? Did every one of them that passed him ask his name? What happened to the money my grandfather gave Mary, whose pockets were empty when her corpse was examined? Of course, John Dunberley took it, and I suggest he used at least part of it to pay those so-called witnesses to stand up and speak against poor, wronged Tom."

Miller and Cousans are silent.

The landlord returns with a decanter and three glasses, though he waits for a nod from Miller before filling one for Rawlinson.

"The way Mary was killed would release a fountain of blood," says Rawlinson quietly as the landlord pours, "and yet on my grandfather's coat they found only three tiny spots – and those on his back – which might easily have come from some pub brawl or butcher's shop."

Cousans harumphs. "All conjecture. All fancy."

"As was the article in your newspaper," Rawlinson retorts.

"What's that children's rhyme?" asks Miller, after tasting his wine. "Sticks and stones may break men's bones, but words will never hurt me."

"But words do hurt," objects Rawlinson. "My mother has tried for many years to have grandfather's conviction overturned. Your sensationalised account of his supposed crime has made that all but impossible. The current view of my grandfather as a cold-blooded killer is now fixed in the public imagination, including that of the judges and lawyers who might have helped us. Whether my grandfather was a good man or a scoundrel I cannot say, since I was deprived of the privilege of knowing him. But whatever he was – rogue, bigamist, womaniser, drunkard – does not matter. He did not kill Mary Kirkham, his trial was a travesty and his awful fate – condemned to hang in that metal cage, to be gawped at and dishonoured as his mortal remains decomposed – was not deserved. That is why I am here, at my mother's request, to ask for your help."

"What can *we* possibly do?" asks Cousans, without interest.

"You could run a sensational exclusive, citing new evidence in this infamous case, and a new suspect," insists Rawlinson. "That would help us obtain my grandfather a pardon, and from a pardon could come a Christian burial of what remains we have of him, which to be truthful is wretchedly little. Let me show you."

Crossing to the table, he unfastens the ribbon on the wooden chest. As he lifts the lid, a faintly noxious odour fills the room, and Miller is transported back to his silent companion on his carriage journey to Lincoln. Though less pungent, the smell is the same.

Rawlinson picks up the box. "As my poor grandfather rotted in his cage, his bones fell to the ground. Some were scavenged by foxes and rats, and others – the larger leg and arm bones for example, and the skull – were claimed by souvenir hunters, to sell or keep as morbid mementoes. But great-grandfather Robert was determined to do what he could to salvage his son's remains. Whenever he could visit the site, he searched the ground beneath the gibbet, crying and lamenting as he dug in the dirt with his bare hands."

The image of the dead man's father crawling around in the mud, digging for his lost son's bones, makes Miller shudder. Rawlinson offers him the box, and glancing inside, Miller is horrified to see a macabre collection of skeletal remnants, among them finger-bones, a shoulder blade, broken ribs and several half-rotted teeth. He gasps in disgust, and turns his face away.

"For God's sake, man! What are these?"

"This pitiful assemblage is all that Robert found," Rawlinson explains, "and preserved carefully in this casket, made with his own hands for the purpose. The box is what we, as his family, fervently wish to have interred in hallowed ground."

But Cousans is shaking his head, "No. I see what you truly want. You're asking us to issue a retraction. Let me tell you, the *Lincoln Chronicle* is not in the business of retractions. Publish a story one week and go back on it the next, people think you're printing garbage. Sales suffer."

"But you *have* printed garbage. My grandfather deserves a pardon and an apology from the authorities, and most of all a proper burial. I've told you Tom Otter's own version of events, and given you the name of Mary Kirkham's real killer. Surely that will sell your newspapers?"

Miller is silent. Cousans drinks his wine.

So Rawlinson adds, quietly, "My mother's afraid he's not at rest. She has seen him. Others have, too."

A chill runs down the back of Miller's neck, as the young man who joined him in his carriage the previous day comes to his mind. Absurd, surely, to connect him with this story?

Cousans barks a laugh. "There you have it, Thomas, the source of this man's complaint. The unbelievable credulity of the lower echelons, with their ghosts and boggarts and things that go bump in the night! His mother believes she's seeing spirits! Well, we are not that kind of publication. The *Chronicle* is a serious newspaper, and will have no involvement with paranormal tales."

"But a Christian burial, Mr Cousans," objects Rawlinson. "Surely you cannot refuse to help the family with that?"

Cousans reaches for the decanter, and refills his glass. "My advice to you, Sir? Take your box of bones, and bury them by night in the churchyard of your choosing. Your relative will sleep soundly, and no one will be any the wiser."

Luncheon is over, Miller's business with Cousans is concluded. But following Cousans's departure, Miller finds his usual appetite for solitude has deserted him. Returning to the reading room, he tries several of the periodicals and journals one after another, but none of them hold his interest. Instead, he finds his thoughts going over his meeting with Rawlinson, doubting the appropriateness of his and Cousans' behaviour.

After a while, Martha brings him tea. She seems subdued.

"You're Walter Rawlinson's relative, aren't you?" asks Miller as she hands him a cup and saucer. "You told him I was staying here."

"Why shouldn't I?" she asks, indignantly. "Is there any law against my speaking of the guests?"

"None whatsoever. But I was taken aback by his intrusion."

"Is it an intrusion, then, to ask you to act decently, in a Christian manner? I judged you to be a kind man, and reasonable, but it seems I am wrong."

She leaves him. Miller finds himself despondent to have lost her good opinion.

Later, upstairs in his room, the erratic fire is again miserly with its heat, yet generous with its billowing smoke. Martha has brought no extra candles; now she never will, and the shadows quivering in the lamplight are oppressive. Again, Miller puts himself to bed, and as before is troubled by the floorboard creaking outside his room, developing a growing conviction that someone stands outside, waiting. As the striking clock marks the second hour of his wakefulness, he climbs huffily from the bed, and carrying the low-burning lamp, throws open the door to demand silence from whoever's out there.

The passage is in darkness. Holding up the lamp, somehow he's unsurprised to find there's no one to be seen.

Before breakfast, Miller sends a boy to cancel his privately-hired carriage, and to reserve him instead an inside seat on the mid-morning mail coach. He explains his decision to himself – not entirely convincingly – that the hotel has been expensive and using public transport will save him money, though a voice in his head acknowledges his reluctance to risk a second encounter with his malodorous companion.

Martha, he's pleased to see, seems to have forgiven him. The mail-coach will be too full to carry all his luggage, but she smiles as she takes his smaller bag for temporary storage and promises she'll make sure it is sent on the following day.

The coach, as expected, is crammed with five others inside besides himself. For once, Miller's pleased to be uncomfortably squashed. No room for any silent young man to take a seat beside him.

Close to the day's end, Miller's housekeeper Dolly Pask prepares a hot toddy, and carries it up to his study. Since his return from Lincoln, he hasn't been himself. Maybe a warming whisky will ward off any illness he might have picked up on his travels.

A fire blazes in the grate, but the lamps are unlit. Miller stands by the window, looking out across the lawn, where against the fading light, a murmuration of starlings swirls. To Dolly's bewilderment, Miller is wearing a woollen cap and gloves as if preparing to go out; but he also appears half-ready to retire in his dressing gown and slippers. Under his dressing gown, she sees his daytime jacket and trousers.

He turns to her. "Ah. It's you, Mrs Pask."

She places the toddy on his desk. "Are you expecting someone, Sir?"

"I wanted to watch the starlings."

His voice seems altered, slower, not his usual direct speech. "But then something caught my eye. Can you see someone under the oak?"

Dolly joins him at the window and looks out. The venerable tree is rooted in the meadow beyond the wall, but its winter-naked branches overhang the rose-bed which in summer is Miller's pride and joy.

The light is in those liminal moments where instead of illuminating, it confounds and confuses. Dolly squints. Is someone there? Is that the brim of a hat, or only the shadows deceiving?

Unnerved, she shakes her head. "I really couldn't say. I hope it's not gypsies again, come to steal the chickens."

Yet the shape she almost sees seems a darker thing than gypsies.

"I'll tell Jed to go and take a look, though he'd better take his shotgun. Are you not feeling well, Mr Miller? I brought you a toddy to brighten you up. Maybe you've taken a chill somewhere on the road."

"Can I show you something?"

Instead of answering her question, he lifts from the desk a paper wrapping bearing a rough scrawl of his name, and picks up a black lacquered box. No bigger than a snuff box, its varnish is deeply scratched with marks Dolly can't interpret exactly but whose inference she can read very well.

"Look." He holds out the box for her to take, but she steps away.

"No, I won't touch it. How do you have this, Sir? Where is it from?"

"It was tucked away inside my bag sent on from Lincoln. Plainly it's not found its way in there by accident, since my name is written on its wrapping. Do you think it is witchcraft?"

Given Miller's obviously disturbed state of mind, Dolly is reluctant to further discompose him.

"I've no belief in that nonsense. Someone's playing a wicked game with you. If I were you, I'd drop it straight in the fire."

"But it has a trick up its sleeve." Miller removes the box's close-fitting lid. An oddly unpleasant odour – faint but still offensive – seeps into the room. Inside, a piece of blue velvet makes a bed for a yellowing piece of bone, which to Dolly appears to be part of a human finger.

In shock, her hands go to her face.

"What a terrible prank to play on a gentleman such as yourself! Who would do such a thing? Someone upset by your writings, no doubt. Throw it in the fire, and come and sit in the parlour a while."

But Miller returns to the window. "He's beckoning to me, though I don't want to go."

"Of course you shan't go. Come and sit by the fire at least, and drink this toddy. I'll go and tell Jed to shoo the blackguard away."

"I'm afraid he won't leave," says Miller, but he allows himself to be led to an armchair, where he sits and takes a sip of the whisky and water.

A paperknife lies on the hearthstone. On the mantelpiece, Dolly notices fresh cuts in the wood, a lattice of lines.

"What's this?" she asks, picking up the knife, pointing to the marks. "What in God's name have you been doing?"

"That's how he'll get in, through the chimney," says Miller, bleakly. "You can block your windows and doors, but the chimney is always open. The symbol may keep him out, but my hopes are not high."

"Mr Miller, Sir," says Dolly, dismayed by his apparent loss of reason, "you're talking of old superstitions, and you such a rational man."

"Did you know I was once a father?" This further swift turn of conversational direction leaves Dolly unsure how to reply. She has heard tales in the village; but Miller is going on. "Many years ago, I was briefly married. And we had a son. He lived only a few hours, but blessedly long enough to be baptised and not condemned to that lost corner of the churchyard where we bury the damned. His name was Arthur. My wife died a few hours after him. They're buried together. We put him in her arms."

"Oh," says Dolly, affected. "I'm very sorry to hear that."

"And I've been thinking, these past few hours, how it would have been if the pastor hadn't been close to hand, and my son's innocent soul had been condemned to hell's fires. How would I ever have lived with myself?"

He drinks again from his toddy. "I have not always been an honourable man, Mrs Pask. But while I was away, I was presented with the opportunity to right a wrong I recently committed. I'm ashamed to say I declined that opportunity, and now I see that I myself am damned. I was blessed always to know where my son was buried, to lay flowers on his grave, knowing that he would spend the afterlife in the care of the angels. I was never so unlucky as to have to dig the earth with my bare hands, searching for my own child's bones."

Now suspecting serious illness, Dolly touches his forehead, expecting to find it hot with fever. Instead, it's icy cold. "You're rambling, Sir. I'll get Jed to go for the doctor. He'll give you something to help you rest."

"Can you see if he's still out there?"

Humouring him, Dolly goes once more to the window.

The light has nearly gone, but what she can see fills her with fear. Beyond doubt someone is there, not under the oak but much closer now, in the middle of the lawn: a young man whose wide-brimmed hat mercifully covers his face.

Saying nothing to Miller, she hurries to the scullery to find Jed.

Jed is finding his shotgun and being too slow – as Dolly keeps telling him – to load it and get himself outside, when they hear the garden door slam.

Dolly runs back to the study. Miller is gone.

Through the window, the night is all but turned to black, though enough light remains to show two dark figures walking side by side across the lawn. Miller appears distressed, both hands covering his face, while his ominous companion keeps one hand firmly on his shoulder, guiding him away.

When they reach the oak tree, they disappear.

Author Comment

I write all kinds of fiction, but my One True Love is crime. I'm pretty much crime obsessed, with a particular passion for true crime and cold cases. So when it came to choosing a folk tale to re-imagine – while I had a really tough time ruling out all the weird and frankly wonderful stories which effectively make up Lincolnshire's supernatural history – the tale of Tom Otter caught my attention and wouldn't let go.

If you haven't read Tom's story, I urge you to do so. The version in general circulation – written over fifty years after Tom's execution – paints him as a vicious murderer, a cruel man and a bigamist who beat his second 'wife' to death while she was eight months pregnant with his child. But from my first reading of the story, my crime-writer's plot-hole detector went into overdrive. I had so many questions! Even allowing for florid embellishments, how could any of the story be true? I came to the conclusion that Tom – though maybe not the best of men – was innocent of this murder.

My novels (under the pen-name Erin Kinsley) are mostly about the effects of serious crime on ordinary families, and how people might cope with the abduction of a child or a daughter's murder. So I decided to think along those lines for the story I've written here. Whatever Tom was, maybe he had a father who loved him, who was there to witness Tom's hanging and watch him hauled up high in the iron cage which imprisoned him for five decades. How could that be borne?

As for Tom himself, if he was innocent, he must also have been filled with unimaginable rage, and a thirst for revenge on those who wronged him. And perhaps he took that revenge in unconventional ways.

YALLERY BROWN

Rory Waterman

I plodded round Chambers' Farm Wood, on the edge
    of a clay-clodded field full of wheat.
The breeze stroked it this way and that, like a hand,
    and the trees shaded me from the heat

of that hushed August day. Oh God, I loved summer,
    but not what it meant I must do:
a farm-hand's life's back-aching toil after back-
    aching toil, all summer day through,

then again, then again. So, rather than cut
    through the wood on my way to the farm,
I was traipsing along with the poppies and hares
    for five minutes, and doing no harm

till I heard a small whine, like a baby that's starting
    to blub, then to cry, then to bawl –
which it did, sure enough. So I climbed through the hedge,
    but I could find nothing at all.

Where is it? *Whose* is it? It must be that Sarah's,
    that sultry lass at number two
who used to spend time with the vicar, but now
    spends most of it drinking Bols Blue –

she must've come down here and left the poor brat,
    I thought. I was wrong. "Gerrit off,"
wheezed a tiny gruff voice. "Gerrit off! Gerrit off!
    Gerrit off! Gerrit off! Gerrit off!"

"Get *what* off, and off *what?*" I said. Then I saw it:
    a small pair of yellow-brown feet
wearing mud boots, then a small mustard head,
    and a rock where the two bits must meet,

so I heaved the rock up in my calloused hands, threw it
    into the brambles, looked down,
and gawped as the fellow jumped up to the height
    of my knees, shouting "Yallery Brown

is back! You've helped me more than you know,
    my lad!" His beard jinked about
like a coil of wet rope, his muddy mud head
    was all wrinkles, and small eyes peeped out,

then darted around, then settled on me.
    "You're a good lad, young Will. Don't be frit.
I know all your dreams involve women and sloth:
    I know you. Say one wish. I'll grant it."

Now, what would you make of this odd little boggart?
    He looked like a gremlin in shrinkwrap,
a Soviet doll left behind at Chernobyl,
    a garden gnome slathered in crap,

and I wished I'd just taken the quick route to work,
    and I wished that it hadn't been me
who'd found him – and maybe I wished that he'd died,
    but he looked quite sincere. In fact, he

repeated his promise then smiled through his beard
    with a skewed grid of yellow-brown teeth.
A combine spewed wheat-dust out three fields away.
    Then he said, "What you let out beneath

that tombstone, my lad, you can't understand,
    and whether you take it or leave it,
that much will stay true. But think: your poor hands" –
    he wank-waved my way – "they are yet

to have some time off. I could give you a wife
    who will love you, somehow. Or your job:
it could all do itself while you sit in the grass,
    or stay home and twiddle your knob.

Just say which you want." It was tempting. I mulled:
    love? There's enough time for love
to sort itself out, so I thought (I was young),
    but no work to do? Lord above!

Maybe I'll go home and surf the net
    for ladies, or go down the pub
and she will be waiting for me, so I thought.
    "Work, please." He nodded, then rubbed

his billiard-ball belly, then nodded again.
    "It's granted!" "Well, thank you," I said,
though not with conviction. He flew in a rage.
    "You *must* never thank me! No shred

of a thank you I'll hear, you grateful young sod!"
    He was flailing and gritting his teeth
and pounding the clods with his clod-coloured boots.
    "Okay!" I cried. Then, with relief,

I saw he was turning to trog on his way,
    and he bounded from molehill to molehill,
but his voice carried back, bringing with it a laugh:
    "Just call when you need me, young Will:

I'm Yallery Brown. Say my name, and I'll come.
    But" – and at this, he looked back –
"don't thank me again, or I'll leave you for good."
    Then the sprightly sprite danced up the track

and out of my life. I stood rubbing my eyes.
    What was *that*? Then I rubbed them again:
my combine was working with nobody in it
    the chute filled the bucket with grain

as it wobbled on past. I jumped through the hedge
    and stood in a field of fresh stubs
where the wheat had all been. Then I tested my luck:
    I walked back to the village, and pub,

and it was a good afternoon. The next day
    I took the short cut to the farm
but got there a few minutes late, and my combine
    was driving itself like a charm,

then it happened again the next day. Then the next
    I just stayed at home and hid,
and the next I forgot, and lounged round the house.
    Then the phone rang. My boss. He was livid.

"Where have you been, you lazy young bastard?
    You're fired if you don't get here *now*!"
"But my work's all been done!" I said proudly. "Well, someone
    has done it! A self-milking cow

I never did see," he stormed, "nor a combine
    that harvests the grain on its own,
though I'm docking the wages of anyone who
    has covered your arse." Then the phone

went dead, so I dressed, and I ran through the wood,
    hollering "Yallery Brown!"
and he skipped out the brush and into my path.
    I slipped to a standstill, looked down,

and brandished my fist (he winked, knowingly)
    and yelped. "What have you started?"
I blurted. "I want my job back! I'll work hard!
    Stop doing my work!" The sprite farted

and giggled his mischievous way, and glared up.
    "Be careful this time what you say."
He morris danced round me, trumping in step.
    "Give me my work back. Today,"

I pleaded. He stopped. "It's granted." "Oh, thank you!"
    I cried out, and sank to the grass,
and at what point I knew my mistake I can't say –
    was it as he thumped my arse

and kicked at my knees, and squealed "I warned you!
    You'll see me no more! Amen!"
or was it as "thank you" hurled out my mouth
    and couldn't be sucked in again?

But he's not been seen since, or at least not by me.
    The farm's doing well, so I hear,
though I'm not allowed back. I watch Jeremy Kyle
    on repeat, have two sprogs, and drink beer,

and tell folk the things I've been telling you now.
    And if you see Yallery Brown
leave him to die, don't ever say thank you,
    run, then find lodgings in town.

Author Comment

We don't know the origins of 'Yallery Brown', but its first written retelling was collected by Marie Clothilde Balfour and published (in approximate local dialect) in *Folklore* in 1891. According to Joseph Jacobs, who retold it in *More English Fairy Tales* (1894), the story had been relayed to Balfour by a farm labourer called Tom, who gave his name to its hapless fully-human protagonist. Jacobs suggests Tom was 'adapting a local legend to his own circumstances'. More recently, Maureen James, in her PhD thesis *Investigating the Legends of the Carrs* (2013), has impressively, and plausibly, traced this man, suggesting he was probably a labourer called Thomas Laming, who worked at a farm near the village of Redbourne.

There are several versions of 'Yallery Brown' in print, all in prose, and some are wonderful. In all cases, though, those versions return us to an otherwise romanticised, unmechanised, bucolic past none of us has ever really experienced. I decided to make the story mine. My protagonist isn't Tom, he is Will: my poem is about my friends William Jackson and, to a lesser extent, Sarah Durrant, and their two kids, Emrys and Francis, and is set in the part of the county where they live. I only hope this all annoys some purse-lipped academic folklorists somewhere. Sadly, it has not annoyed William or Sarah.

Ballad stanzas energised by a rollicking anapaestic metre just felt right for what is in a sense a beautifully daft tale – albeit one that also concerns contemplation of several of the

Deadly Sins and the unlikely results of submitting to one of them. I dread (i.e. smile) to think what Balfour and Jacobs might think of my rendition. Writing this poem inspired me to produce modern-world versions of several other folk tales, which are included in my collection *Come Here to This Gate* (Carcanet, 2024). 'Yallery Brown' was first published in that collection, and is republished here with the kind permission of Carcanet Press.

THE DEAD HAND AND A POTTLE O' BRAINS
(A CUT-UP AND ALPHABETIZATION EXERCISE BASED ON TWO M. C. BALFOUR MANUSCRIPTS)

Daniele Pantano

A: "A can that," says she. "A disna like the job," an' he took oot a knife an' felt 's edge. "A reckon a 's fo't 'e the reet thing to last," says he, "thoff a hevn't azac'ly cut th' heart oot, it be so moocky wark." "A reckon thon 's too hard for wimmen fo'ak." "A reckon thou'lt do then 's weel 's anybody," says he. "A've lost tha on'y twae things as a cared for, an' what else can a fin' to buy a pottle o' brains wi'!" an' he fair howled, till tha tears ran doun into 's mooth. "An' a 've suthin' else to see to," says she, "so gode'en to 'ee," and she carried the pot away wi' her into tha back place. "An' mappen 't 'ull no," says he, an' looked out o' the window. "An' men' ma clouts?" says he. "An' reckon a 'll hev to kill that pig," says he, "fur a like fat bacon better nor iverythin'." "An' scrub?" says he. "An' what 's yaller an' shinin', but isna goold?" "An' – an'," says he, 'n comes to a stop, "a reckon we'll tackle business noo, hevin' done tha perlite like." "An' – an' – tha beasts is fattenin'," says he. "An' hevna thee anybody to look arter thee?" "Ay, a can," says she. "Aye so"? says tha wise woman, "a' might manage that, ef so be thou'll help thysel'." "Aye so?" says she, an' looked at him through her spec'itals. "Aye," says she, an' went on stirring. A

149

can't sa'ay if they be all true; but a wudn't loike to sa'ay 'at
they be'nt. A reckon theer wor quare things to than, an'
mappen, fur all a knows, jest 's quare aboot 's to year; ony w'er
growed too gran' to seen un. A'll cum back sa'afe 'n soun' bye
'n bye; don't tha be a fool loike tha rest o' um, dost hear?" A's
back wor bent, an' 's limbs wor shakin' loike an au'd gran'ther,
's gre'at bla'azin' eyne glared in 's whoite wrinkled fa'ace, an'
's hair, as 'd bin so bra'oun 'n co'ly, wor hangin' i' long wisps
o' whoite 'n gray ivery wa'ays to wanst. A've heerd tell as wan
creepit oop th' pad on 's han's an' kneebo'ans, an' another wor
fun' layin' in a watter-ho'al, an' so, by 'n by, th' foak as'd coom
doon fro' th' toon, got 'em ahl oot. Ah! – an' none iver knowed
what a *did* see, or what a'd seed ahl th' awfull noights 'n da'ays,
as 'd doolt wi' th' horrors, none iver knowed wheer a'd bin, or
what wa'ay a coom back, more'n tha bleedin' stump cud tell
um of a stroogle an' a tooggin' fur dear loife, wi' th' ahful Han',
fur Long Tom Pattison niver spo'ak a wo'd agin, arter a wor
fun' by th' snag, wi's mother croonin' an' fondlin' aboot un.
Ahl da'ay long a'd sit i' th' sun, or by th' foire, grinnin' an'
girnin'; an' ahl noight long, a 'd wan'ner roon th' edge o' th'
Cars, screechin' an' moanin' loike a thing i' torment, wi' 's pore
au'd mother follerin' loike a dog at heel, beggin' an' prayin' un
to coom ho'am, 'n 'if won o' 's au'd ma'ates 'd stop to look at
un, 's mother 'd sa'ay – pattin' th' he'ad o' th' pore silly creetur
– "A *said* a'd coom hoam, an' a did; ma babby did acoom
ho'am to 's mother, 'n she a widder woman!" An by'n by tha
door wor flinged open, 'n oot he cam' laughin' loike mad, an'
pullin' awa'ay fro's au'd mother, as wor tryin' to put suthin' in

's pocket, an' greetin' fit to break her heart. An they 'gan to wun'ner if, arter all, th' lad ra'aly meant to cross th' Cars alo'an. An' a can't ra'ly tell 'ee what'n a wa'ay tha wor got oot o' tha ter'ble bogs. An' a sna'atched tha la'anthorn fra th' au'd woman, an' runn'd aff a-aughin' 'n floutin' th' la'ads, t'ords the Car'en'. An' a spak so bould an' easy-loike that some o' th' youngsters 'gun to think 'at mebbe a wor reet arter all, 'n that tha bogles wor no'on so bla'ack, 's th' sa'ayin' is, 's tha wor pa'inted. An' ahl da'ay long, the au'd woman wan'ered aboot th' Cars, ca'allin' an' ca'allin' on her son to coom ba'ack, coom back to 's mother, 'n she a widder! An' as he said that, he thowt of the words o' the wise woman. An' as tha stood waitin' an' wonnerin' tha seed tha au'd mother scurryin' along o' th' pad t'ords un, beckonin' 'n wavin' loike mad. An' as they comed oop the pad, she wor sittin' at the door, twinin' straws. An' closer 'n closer tha coom roond La'ang To'am as a stood wi 's ba'ack agen tha sna'ag an 's ha'ands in 's pockets, tryin' to keep 's heart oop. An' doun she sets by him, an' he tellt her all aboot the wise woman an' the pig, an' 's mother an' the riddles, an' 'at he was alo'an i' the warld. An' ef a rued it, a mun gi'n oop floutin' at ither fo'aks fur gittin' fe'ared i' th' da'arklins; "Begox," said th' silly creetur, "a'l not rue from ma wo'd, a promise 'ee. An' ef a should dee, who'd take care o' a poor fool such 's thou, no more fit to look arter thysel' than an unborn babby? but min' thy manners, an' speak her pretty, my lad: fur they wise fo'ak are gey'an light mispleased." An' he scratched 's head, an' thowt, an' thowt, but a couldna tell. An' he scratched 's head, an' twisted 's hat. An' ivery wan said as he

'd rue 't some da'ay, an 's mother wor allus beggin' an' prayin'
un to carry wan wi' un as she 'd got fro' au'd Molly, the wise
woman as doolt gainhan' to th' mill. An' noight arter noight
thur wor a la'amp flarin' in th' winder o' th' cottage at th' lane
en', an' th' au'd mother sat theer waitin' on her bo'oy, an' tha
door stud open fro' tha darklins' to tha dawnin'. An' o' noights
he 'd mock at th' men-fo'ak 'case they wor feared o' th'
darklins, an' he 'd mak' oot as he seed things i' tha black
corners, so 's to set them skeereder nor iver. An' oop came a
lass as lived gainhand, an' looked at un. An' presently, tha
sa'aid efter'rds, tha heerd To'am shoutin' an' sweer'n' as tha
bla'ack things cum clo'aser 'n clo'aser, so 's tha cud on'y
glimpse um now an' tha'an, an' then's 's arms wor thrown oop
an' a 'pear'd to be foightin' an' strooglin' wi tha things aboot
um, an' bye an' bye tha cud hear nobbut th' skirlin', la'affin',
'n wa'ailin', an' moanin' o' th' horrors, an' tha cud see nobbut
th' shiftin' bla'ackness o' tha crowdin' shapes, till a'al to wanst
tha da'arkness open'd oot an' straight afore um they seed Long
To'am sta'anin' by tha sna'ag, 's fa'ace 's whoite 's de-ath an'
starin' eyne, holdin' on wi wan ha'an to tha willa an' wi th'
other stretch'd oot an' cla'asp'd in a ha'an wi' oot a body, as
pulled un an' pulled un wi' a dreadful strongness t'ords tha
bla'ack bog beyont th' pa'ad. An' she clapt the book togither,
an' t'orned 's back. An' she kept 's house so clean an' neat, an'
cooked 's dinner so fine, 'at one night a says to her: "Lass, a 'm
thinkin' a like thee best o' iverything, arter all." An' tha cud
see 'at tha loight as flickered on Tom's fa'ace coom fro' tha
Dead Han' itsel, wi th' rottin' flesh droppin' off tha mouldy

bo'ans, an' its dreadful fingers grippin' tight hol' o' Tom's han', 'zif tha wor growed together. An' tha *do* tell 's Long Tom niver rested in 's pla'ace i' th' kirkgarth, an' that o' dark noights afore th' Cars wor dra'ained, a want moanin' oop an' doon by th' edge o' th' bog, wi' 's au'd mother trailin' efter 'm, an' i' mid o' th' shriekin' an' sobbin' fo'ak said as tha cu'd hear tha au'd woman's voice, whimperin' oot, as 'd done so often i' li'fe: "A coom back to 's mother, 'n she a widder!" An' tha silly lad, as 'd mebbe took more beer 'n he 'd oughter, fired oop, an' swore as a feared nowt, seen or unseen, an' a 'd cross th' Cars wi' nobbut a lanthorn o' th' da'arkest noight o' th' year. An' than, tha things 'at To'am wor so onbeleevin' about, tha'ay coomed, tha'ay did – th' horrors o' th' air, an' th' horrors o' th' watters, an' tha slimy, creepin' things, an' th' cryin' wa'ailin' things – till tha noight, as 'd bin so quiet 'n still, wor full o' movin' shadows an' dim girnin' fa'aces wi' bla'azin' eyne 'n wa'ailin' voices. An' the fool scratched 's head, an' thowt, an' thowt; but a couldna tell. An' the lass whispered in 's ear: "It be a tadpole." An' whan a wor de'ad th' women took 's mother awa'ay, an' tried to kep' a fro' gittin' ba'ack to un. An' when he got in, 's mother ony looked at un, an' smiled, 's if to say she could leave un wi' a quiet min, sence a'd got brains 'nuff noo to look arter 's sel' – an' then she dee'd. An' wi' that she nodded to 'em, an' up and into the house. And' theer a sat, gibbering, girnin', an' grinnin' at th' horrors, as nobbut hisself cud see! Anyways – a wudn't loike to do 's Long Tom Pattison did, 'case a mout come to th' sa'ame en'. Ay – that's ahl theer wor of it; it's not much of a story—but seest tha, 't ahl coom o' 's onbelievin' ways, as led un into 't to fust. Ay, an' a ha seed un masel', bits o' paper wi' varses oot o' th' Bible, crinkled oop in a nutshell; three straws 'n a clover leaf tied wi hair off of a dead man; or mebbe the clippins o' a dead wumman's nails, ef a cud get un. Ay, the Cars wor a fearsome pla'ace i' they da'ays if all ta'ales be true.

B: "But see here." "But thou 'll hev' to read me a riddle so 's a can see thou 'st brought the reet thing, an' ef thy brains is 'boot thee." "But what 'll a do 'bout this wise woman?" "But," says he, scratching his head, "hoo can a do that?" But as a got nigh the hoose, oot came fo'ak runnin' to tell un 'at 's mother was deein'. But fur all that th' men an' lads met at th' corner o' th' green lane, agin the cottage wheer a doolt wi's mother, cum the da'arklins. But he on'y laughed, an' niver a safe-keep would a hev. But I hev heerd mony a stra'ange thing aboot un as 'd make thy sking creep to harken to. But i' ma toime, 'twor mostly Bible-spells or varses writ by a wise woman 'n sich-loike. But ma faith! what 'n 'a cha'anged creetur a wor! But ne'er a tra'ace o' tha lad cud a fin'. But o' th' fa'ace o' him, ah, theer wor 'n *ahful* look, 's if th' horrors 'd follored un an' fott un fur ther o'an. But on tha went, Long To'am mebbe thu'ty ya'ards ahead, singin' an' whistlin' 's bould 's cud be, an' behoind, tha la'ads, keepin' clo'ase t'gither, but gettin' less feared as tha got furder 'n furder into th' Cars, wi'oot seein' owt o' tha bogles 'n tha horrors. But th' au'd uns know'd better'n that, an' shuk ther he'ads, an' wished 'at no ha'arm 'd cum o' th' boy's folly an' onbelievin' wa'ays. But tha creetur tore awa'ay from un, loike a mad thing, an' rin back to th' Cars, an' 'gun ca'allin' 'n ca'allin' on her son, jist 's afore, to cum back to 's poor lone mother, 'n she a widow. But tha lads wor fair oot o' ther wits wi' fear, an' tha cudn't tell what 'd coom o' Long Tom. But tha nex' da'ay, when they heerd ahl aboot 'un, th' fo'ak went, nat'rally i' th' good sun loight, into th' Cars, an' tha sowt, an' sowt fur Long Tom, an' 's poor au'd mother ca'alled an' cried on 'un, an' swore 'at a cudna live wi'oot her on'y son, her babby, an' she a pore widder woman. But tha niver ha'armed un 'case of their safe-keeps an' ther prayers; but tha howled at un, an' ploocked at un, till tha pore things wor cle'an mazed wi' froight, an' sick wi' tha a'afulness o' it. But tha wor no' so sure o' ther-sels, an' wor skeery enuff whe'en tha fa'and th' squishy yarth unner foot, an' saw tha glint o' tha lanthorn fa'allin' on tha bla'ack watter hoals, gain ha'and to th' pa'ad. But Tom on'y la'aughed agean, an' snappit 's fingers i' Willy's fa'ace. But wan noight at th' inn th' men-bodies to'ned on th' lad, an' said as he wor main ready to get 's fun oot o' them, but fur all that he worn't no'on better nor th' rest of 'um, when 't cum to maddlin' wi' th' bogles, or crossin' th' Cars to evens i' tha darklins. But when tha want to put th' lad in 's coffin fur th' buryin', theer she wor, stoock oop i' th' co'ner of th' bed, wi' him i' her a'arms, nussin' un as 'd used to do while a wor a tiddy thing, an' de'ad – de'ad – loike tha son upo' her knees.

C: "Can thee so?" says he, doubtful like. "Can'st cook?" says he. "Canst tell me what that be, as has first nae legs, an' then twae legs, an' en's wi' fower legs?" "Coom, us 'll go oop to the wise woman towanst," and off they went. "Could thee do 't?" says he.

D:—

E: Efter that th' lads cud sca'arce tell what hapt wi 'em.

F: "Faix, it be!" says he. "Fine," says he. Fo'ak tellt him as he could get everything a liked from tha wise woman as lived on the top o' the hill, an' dealt in potions an' herbs an' spells an' things, an' could tell thee all as 'd come to thee or thy folk. Fo'ak wor geyan skeered o' gruesome things an' 'ud niver goa oot o' noights alo'an by thersels. Fur wi' all s' tricks, a wor a decent lad, on'y too full o' 's fun, an' too waggle-headed to min' what a wor doin' most toimes.

G: "Go thy ways," says she, "thou'st no fo't me the reet thing yet." "Gode'en, fool," says she. "Gode'en, missis," say he, "a 've brought thee tha heart o' tha thing a likes best o' all; an' a put it hapt i' paper on tha table." "Gode'en, missis," says he, "a reckon a 've fo't 'ee the reet thing this time, surely," an' he plumped the sack down kerflap! on the doorsil. "Gode'en, missis," says he. "Good e'en, missis," says he, "its a fine night."

H: "Hev 'a got to kill thee, dost think, an' take thy heart oop to the wise woman for that pottle o' brains?" "Hev' ye ony brains fur to sell?" "Hi, yi!" says he, "must a cut oot mother's heart an' tak' it to her?" "Hout no," says he, "jist ord'nar brains – fit fur any fool – same 's everyone has 'bout here; su'thin' clean common-like." Hawiver, as tha coom nigh tha willa-snag, th' win' coom oop tha valley, wi' a la'ang soughin' moa-an – chill 'n da'amp a coom'd fro' th' sea – wa'ailin' 's if a carried wi' 't a'ahl th' evil thin's as dool i' th' da'arkness an' tha shadows. He minded hoo she'd nuss't un when a wor a tiddy brat, an' he'ped un wi' 's lessons, an' cooked 's dinners, an' mended 's clouts, an' born wi' 's foolishness: an' a felt sorrier 'n' sorrier, while a began to sob an' greet. He scratched 's head, an' thowt, an' thowt, but a couldn't tell. Her wor a wild slip of a lad, allus in mischeèf, nobody 'd an evil wo'd agin un. Hoo 's that fur, missis?" says he. Howiver, some o' th' youngsters thought sha'ame t' be feared, seein' as Tom recked nowt o' th' horrors, an' mebbe a dozen o' um follered un down th' pa'ad 's led to th' Cars.

I: "I doubt thou's a bigger fool nor a thought!" an' shut the door in 's face. "I'se no'on brains fur 'ee to-day." "In thy wife's head," says she. "It do," says he, an' scratched 's head. "It'll mebbe rain," says he, an' fidgetted from one foot to t'other. In th' inn o' evens all th' men-fo'ak 'ud wait, wan upon other, while tha cud all go ho'am togither; an' even then, tha misloiked tha shadows an' tha da'ark corner-pla'aces, an' fingered ther safe-keeps all th' wa'ay ho'am.

J: "Jest so," says she, lookin' in 's pot: "bring me the heart o' tha thing thou likes best o' all, an' a 'll tell thee where to get thy pottle o' brains." "Jist thou take me 's a be, heart 'n all, 'n a wager a 'll help thee read the riddles."

K:—

L: "Laws, no!" says she, lookin' skeered, "a winna hev' that."

M: "Mappen," says he then, "it mout be a tadpole, missis." "Mappen," says she. "Mebbe," says she. "Mebbe," says the wise woman, "but read me this, noo, what's yaller an' shinin' but isna goold?"

N: "Naw," says he, "an' a canna buy my pottle o' brains fur nuthin' a like best lef'!" "Naw; but if a had, mebbe a'd a got my pottle o' brains," says he. "No! a can't do 't," says he. "No'a, mother, a tell tha," tha lad wor sa'ayin', "a'l hev none o' tha spells 'n bobberies; stop tha whimperin', wilt tho'." "Not a bit o't," says she. Niver heerd on un? ooh, a'l can thee 'bout *that*, an' a reckon *that's* a true ta'ale hawiver. Noa, a didn't live more'n aboot a year, mappen.

O: "Oh, mother, mother!" says he, "who'll tak' care on me noo!" "Oh, wait a bit," says she, "suthin' mowt turn up, an' it 'll no matter ef thou 'rt a fool, s' long 's thou'st got me to look after thee." "Oo a's killed ma pig, 'n lost my mother, an' a'm nobbut a fool mysel'," says he, sobbin'. "Ou, ay!" says she, "fo'ak says as fools mak' good husban's, an' a reckon a'll hev thee, ef thou'st willin'." Oh, tha' wor sort o' spells loike; nigh ivery wan had suthin' to ke'p th' evil things off, an' ma father ha' tould ma on many as a 'd seed. Once i' these parts, an' not so long gone nayther, there was a fool as wanted to buy a pottle o' brains, for he was iver gettin' into scrapes through his foolishness, an' bein' laughed at by iveryone. Oot we'ent To'am's la'anthorn, an' sich'n a skeery so'ort o' chill cum wi' th' soughin' win', 'at th' la'ad stop't 's singin' 'n sto'od stock still by tha willa-sna'ag. Ower 'n ower agin a cried 'n wailed arter a' son, an' tha cud do nowt to hush a'.

P: Pack o' fools as y' are, what fur shu'd a cum to ha'arm i' th' Cars, wheer a mun goa nigh ivery da'ay in ma reg'lar wo'k?"

Q:—

R:—

S: "See there!" says he, an' sets doun by tha road side an' greets. "Surely," says she. So 'e thowt an' thowt, an' next day 'e went an' borrowed a sack, an' bundelt 's mother in, an' carried it on 's showther up to th' wise woman's cottage. So doun 'e sat, an' the more 'e thowt aboot it the badder 'e feeled. So 'e killed 's pig, an' nex' day off 'e went to tha wise woman's cottage, an' there she sat, readin' in a great book. So 'e tellt 's mother, 'n axed her if 'e should seek tha wise woman 'n' buy a pottle o' brains. So off goes the fool to 's mother, an' tellt her what tha wise woman said. So off 'e went after 's tea, an' there she was, sittin' by tha fire, an' stirrin' a big pot. So off tha fool went to tell 's mother. So th' au'd fo'ak waggled ther he'ads an' went hoam hopin' fur th' best, but feelin' sore mischancy. So tha da'ays want on, an' 'twor m' seventh even sence Tom 'd bin dra'agged into th' ma'ashes, when all to wanst jist afore th' da'arklins, th' fo'ak sa'anterin' by th' edge o' th' Cars, as a 'd took to doin' since th' lad 'd bin lost, well, th' fo'ak heerd a gre'at cry, 'n agean a great cry, so full o' wunner 'n joy, 'at it wor sort o' gruesome to ha'arken to 't. So tha mum le'ave her alo'an, fur tha cud fin' nowt o' tha lad, an' as th' da'ays went on th' fo'ak want to ther wo'k agin, an' th' boys as 'd follored Tom into th' ma'ashes crep aboot scared 'n whoite 'n tremlin', an' a'd amost think as iverythin' wor th' sa'ame as 'd bin afore, but Tom 'd niver coom back. So they went ho'am together, an' a niver wanted to buy a pottle o' brains age'an, fur 's wife 'ad enuff fur both. Stronger 'n stronger it pulled, 'an to last tha lad gi'n oop 's hold, an' wor dragged fro' tha snag an' off tha pad, an' shriekin' wi' a great cry, loike mebbe a sowl in hell, a wor swallered oop i' tha da'arkness.

T: 'Twor a bit skeery, but nath'eless, off tha went arter a, so fa'ast as ther bo'ans 'd tak 'um, oot into th' ma'ashes, an' oop to th' willer-snag, an' theer, while tha ca'ht oop wi' a, sat Long Tom, wi 's back agin th' snag, an' 's feet i' th' watter! 'Twor afore my toime. "Tell 's the first 'un." "Tell me this then, what rins wi'oot feet?" "Tha do'ant knaw what mowt 'appen to tha." "That 's no 'on fur me to say," says she, "fin' oot fur thysel', my lad! ef thou disna want to be a fool a' thy days." "That 's

reet," says she, "an' thou'st got thy pottle o' brains a'ready."
"That depen's," says she, "ef thou wants king's brains, or
sodger's brains, or schoolme'aster's brains, a dinna keep 'em."
"*That* fur tha boggart, an' thee to'oa!" "That ye should," says
she: "thou'st sore need o' them, my son." "That's bad," says
he. "That's good hearin'," says she, "an' what then?" "That's
true," says he, an' off tha went and got married. "The crops is
gittin' on fine." "The on'y cure fur a fool 's a good wife to look
arter 'n, an' that thou'st got; so gode'en to 'ee!" "Then do 't,
my lad," said 's mother, "fur sartain 't 'ull be a stra'ange an'
good thing fur 'ee, ef thou canst buy a pottle o' brains, an' be
able to look arter thy ain sel'." "They are," says she. "Thou
didn't cut oot thy mother's heart, did tha?" "Thou shouldn't
hev lef' me alo'an, fur a liked thee better nor iverything!"
"Thou'st no hit the reet thing, my lad," says she. Th' horrors
cum roond um, an' skirled an' flouted 'em. Tha boys ahoind
wor wuss nor him, tha dars'nt goa ba'ack an' tha dars'nt goa
forra'd, tha cud on'y stan' trem'lin' an' prayin' 'n holdin' on to
ther sa'afe-keeps i' th' da'arkness, an' waitin' fur suthin' ta
'appen. Tha fo'ak said as how she wor smilin' loike a babby
sleepin'. Tha foak wor sort o' skeered on her, an' 'd git oot o's
wa'ay to let her go by, fur a flitted aboot loike wan o' th' bog
things thersel's, a wor so grey 'n bent 'n wrinkled 'n sorrowful.
Tha la'ads ahoind un, wor on ther knee-boanes by ne'ow,
prayin' for dear loife, an' ca'allin' on tha sa'aints an' th' Vargin
an' tha wise wimmen to sa'ave um; but tha cud see as To'am
wor sta'an'in' wi 's ba'ack agen the sna'ag, an' seed 's whoite
fa'ace an' angry eyne thruff tha throngin' shadows atween um.

Tha men, some of un, tried t' stop th' la'ad, an' begged un not to goa, seest tha? an' Willie Kirby sa'aid: "A'll rue ma wo'ds ef tha do'a-ant rue thine; an' tha can flout 's so much as thee loikes, on'y sta-ay by, 'n do'ant goa yonner." Tha very da'arkness seemed aloive wi' un, an' th' air wor thick wi' ther wa'ailin'. Tha women tuk th' au'd mother ba'ack to th' cottage, an' tried to comfort her 'n hush her greetin'. *That* wor a main good safe-keep, a ha' heered sa'ay. The wise woman looked at 'em both, an' wiped her spec'itals. The wise woman nodded 's head. Theer a sat, wi' 's mother greetin' ower un, an' kissin' ivry bit o' un by to'ns. Theer wor nigh a row at th' inn that noight, but to last they ca'almed thersel's doon a bit, an' 'twor sattled as Long Tom 'ud goa by tha pad 'cross tha Car' en', an' round by tha willow-snag on th' verry nex' noight 's iver wor.

U:——

V:——

W:——What?——"Weel," says he, "a can't min' nuthin' else aboot tha weather, but lemme see. "Weel," says she, "a wouldn't min' lookin' arter thee mysel'." "Wel," says she, "let 's see noo." "What art ta'alkin' aboot!" says she. "What rins wi' oot feet?" says he. "What'll a do! what'll a do to get that pottle o' brains, noo a'm alone i' the worl'?" "What's oop wi' thee, fool?" says she. "Wheer be they?" says he, lookin' aboot, an' feelin' in 's pockets. "Why, the sun!" says she. "Why, watter!" says she. Wal, Long Tom wor nigh th' on'y man i' th' pla'ace as 'd niver a safe-keep at all. Wan they got theer tha cud hear tha au'd woman sobbin' an' scoldin' i' th' kitchen. Well, nex' da'ay, they all thowt as Tom 'd rue 's wo'd soon's a'd thowt on it a bit. Well, to than, as a said afore, theer wor he'aps o' ta'ales aboot, of boggarts 'n horrors 'n sich, a cayn't tell thee reetly what all. What? Wheniver tha fo'ak axed wheer a mowt be, tha 'gun to screech an' sob wi' terror, so tha cud get nuthin' oot o' th' critters that noight. Wi' wan han', a kep' p'intin', p'intin' at suthin', an' starin' at suthin', 's if a seed nowt else; an' whur th' other han' 'd oughter bin, th' han' as 'd bin gript by th' dreadful Dead Fingers – ther wor nobbut a ragged bleedin' stump – th' han' 'd bin pulled clean off!

X:—

Y:—

Z:—

Author Comment

'The Dead Hand and a Pottle o' Brains' represents both an exercise in conceptual poetics and an exploration of Walter Benjamin's notions of 'pure language' and 'interruption [as] one of the fundamental devices of all structuring.' The process of writing this new tale began with the transcription of two original folk tales recorded by M. C. Balfour in 'Legends of the Lincolnshire Cars' (1891): 'The Dead Hand' and 'A Pottle o' Brains'. Upon the completion of the transcription, I cut the tales into individual sentences and then restructured the resultant textual material into a new form by ordering the sentences in alphabetical order and organising these fragments via twenty-six paragraphs, using the letters of the alphabet. As such, this new and mutated folk tale allows for interpretation, narrative, and meaning to be made, re-made, transformed, imagined, and reimagined with every reading.

THE BOGGART HAD SEEN IT BEFORE

Juliet E. McKenna

"It must be my fault. I'm so sorry." Anxious, Jacob swept chestnut hair back from his forehead. "It's just that you've said so often how you need peace and quiet to write. I thought this is what we'd agreed. That's why you brought your laptop, isn't it? To work on your novel? They're expecting me back at work today. No, look, I can ring in—"

"Don't do that." Olivia felt sick with embarrassment as they stood in the farmhouse's hall. "It's just a misunderstanding. It really doesn't matter. Seriously. Anyway, you're right. It'll be great to do some writing without any interruptions."

"As long as you're sure?" Jacob hesitated on the front step, tossing his car keys from hand to hand. "I could ask for a week's unpaid leave."

"I'm sure," Olivia said firmly. "Go on. You don't want to be late."

"Okay." The crease between Jacob's eyebrows eased and he smiled, as charming as ever. "Make the most of your day, darling. You deserve it. I'll see you this evening."

He walked quickly out to the Audi, and waved to her as he drove away. Standing in the porch, Olivia watched the tail-end of the car disappear around the curve of the lane. She lowered her hand and drew a deep breath. She had honestly thought they would be spending this whole fortnight together, not just the first week. On the other hand, it was true she lamented often enough how hard it was to find time to write while she was working a full-time job.

The varnished front door stood open behind her. Olivia went back into the house. A passing gleam of sunlight warmed the dark oak panelling on the walls to glossy brown. As she closed the door the draft sent a stray leaf skittering across the patterned tile floor. Jacob had said the geometric border in blue, cream, black and ochre had been part of the Victorian refurbishment. The house had been in his family for centuries. His grandparents had farmed the rich black soil of these lowlands overlooked by the Lincolnshire Wolds. Jacob had told her how he visited every summer holiday as a child. His mother had married while she was still at university and his father's job had taken them to the south coast.

He had made the place sound idyllic. To be fair, it pretty much was, especially if you had grown up on a 1970s housing development on the edge of Birmingham, close to the factories where most of your relatives worked. This lovely old house was surrounded by flat green fields criss-crossed with hedgerows, and reaching to the horizon.

Olivia walked through the hall, passing the open study door on her left and the drawing room on her right. She tried to remember their conversation in the bar when Jacob had invited her here. How could she have made such a stupid mistake? Though the bar had been incredibly noisy. She must have misheard him, or he had misheard her. It didn't really matter, did it? It was just a misunderstanding.

She went on past the stairs and the sitting room, and into the big kitchen. You wouldn't know it was there, coming down the drive from the narrow road. The front of the house looked like a child's drawing. The porch in the centre of the dappled pink bricks had a single window on either side and three bedroom windows were evenly spaced above them. Jacob's prosperous nineteenth-century ancestors had turned the house into an L-shape by adding this extension for a smaller kitchen, scullery and wash house, with extra bedrooms above. His parents had knocked everything through to make this luxurious kitchen-diner when they had retired here.

It was such a shame they hadn't had longer to enjoy it. Jacob had told her what happened with tears in his hazel eyes. The pandemic… These past few years had been so hard. Still, whenever he came here, he felt his mum and dad were with him. As if they were just out of sight, out of hearing, in another room. He was certain they would have loved Olivia. He liked to think that they knew, somehow, how happy she had made him.

She filled the kettle and switched it on. Truth be told, she could use this unexpected free time to catch up on a few other things besides writing. She owed Lucy an answer to what must be a week's worth of texts, and she knew she'd missed calls from Amy and Caitlin. Honestly, she and the girls had hardly seen each other since Jacob had matched with her on that dating app. Not a day had gone by without him sending her cute messages and pictures. Every Friday when she got home, beautiful flowers arrived with a card telling her where he had booked their table for dinner on Saturday and where he was taking her for Sunday brunch.

Taking her mobile out of her jeans' back pocket, Olivia swiped the screen and frowned. She had given up hope of a signal here on their first day. Jacob had apologised for not mentioning the house was a phone not-spot before they arrived. He was so used to it, that had never occurred to him. Still, as he said, everyone deserved to unplug and switch off when they were out of the office, especially someone as dedicated to their job as Olivia. She could hardly argue with that.

But the broadband had been working fine. Jacob had used it to book tables at charming local pubs and restaurants. After days of long country walks in the glorious spring sunshine, and those wonderful meals out, they had spent their evenings snuggled on the sofa in the sitting room, watching romantic comedies on Netflix. Then they'd gone upstairs to bed, where Olivia had enjoyed the best sex she could have imagined. Admittedly, she didn't have much basis for comparison.

Now though, her phone screen blithely announced there was 'No Internet Connection'. Hopefully a quick reset should sort that out. Where was the router? Olivia looked around. It wasn't in the kitchen. She didn't remember seeing it in the sitting room, but she went to check anyway. She was right. It wasn't in the drawing room either, or the study. Olivia walked back into the tiled hall and headed upstairs. She couldn't find it in any of the bedrooms either.

She went back to the kitchen, puzzled. She'd have to ask Jacob when he got home from work. So much for sharing her happiness with Amy, Cait and Lu. Oh well, never mind. When she got back, they'd arrange a girls' night out and catch up properly. It really had been too long. In the meantime, she should start some writing. Jacob was bound to ask how much she had got done. He always wanted to know every detail of her day, however dull it had been. Olivia stuck her phone back in her pocket and made herself a mug of instant coffee.

A sudden thud was shockingly loud in the silence. Olivia spilled half her coffee onto the quarry-tiled floor. Her heart racing, she put the mug in the sink and rinsed her hand under the tap. Reaching for a tea towel, she tried to work out what the noise could have been. She swallowed hard as she realised she hadn't locked the front door. Could someone have sneaked in? Had a prowler realised she was on her own, miles from the nearest village? No one would hear her screams as she fought for her life like the last blonde in a horror movie…

Olivia drew a deep breath, and started opening kitchen drawers as quietly as she could. To her surprise, most of them were empty. As she searched, she snatched glances into the hall. Finally finding a marble rolling pin and moving to the doorway, she stood for a few moments and listened hard. Nothing. She took a few noiseless steps and looked into the sitting room with the comfy sofa and the telly. No one was in there. No one could have gone upstairs either. She would have heard the ancient wooden treads creaking.

She went around the corner, clutching the cold rolling pin. The front door was still shut. The picture-hung drawing room was empty. There was nothing to see in the study either. No, that wasn't quite right. A book lay on the floor. She walked into the room and looked at the tightly-packed bookcase against the wall facing the window. The gap was easy enough to see, as obvious as a missing tooth. Olivia picked the book up, though she couldn't work out how it could have fallen to the floor.

However it had happened, that was the sound she had heard. She put the rolling pin down on the old desk under the window that looked out down the drive. Somehow the book had landed open, face down on the floor. It was one of those old hardbacks with the pages stitched into it. The writing on the blue cloth of the spine was so faded Olivia couldn't make out the title or the author, but the front cover was better preserved. She could read 'Traditional Lincolnshire Folk Tales by the Reverend Octavius Bradshaw, MA Cantab.'

Olivia started reading at the open page. 'The Black Lady of Bradley Woods' turned out to be a tragic ghost haunting some woodland in the north-east of the county, close to the Humber. Her husband had been dragged off by some lord to fight in the Wars of the Roses. He must have been killed because he never came home. The young widow and her baby were left alone and undefended. Three enemy soldiers caught her out walking one day. They raped her, and stole her baby. Distraught, the poor woman wandered the woods every day until she died of grief. Her ghost continued searching for her lost child ever after.

Olivia grimaced. "So much for the good, old days."

Her words rang through the empty house. She really hadn't meant to say that aloud. Olivia closed the book and put it back on the shelf. She really should start writing. She turned the key in the front door lock before she went upstairs to fetch her laptop, and settled on the sitting room sofa.

Out here, it felt strange to be writing an intricate family saga set in the multicultural streets of 1960s Birmingham. Still, Jacob was right. Once she got started, Olivia found she was writing quickly and fluently. She grabbed a sandwich for lunch and carried on. She was so absorbed that she didn't notice time passing. Then a fist banging on the front door broke the spell.

"Olivia!" Jacob shouted. "Where are you? Let me in!"

"Shit." Looking up, she remembered she had left the front door key in the lock. She hurried to let him in. "Sorry, sorry. I was on my own, so—"

"It doesn't matter." He forced a smile and raised the shopping bags he was holding. "I thought we'd eat in tonight. I'll cook."

"Oh, right. Thanks." She took the bag he held out and followed him into the kitchen.

"So, how did you get on?" He put his shopping on the counter above the dishwasher.

"Really well," Olivia admitted with a grin.

"Read me something while I'm cooking."

"Oh, no. This is just the first draft so it's very rough."

"I'll help you polish it up." Jacob took two wine glasses out of a cupboard. "We're not going to let those bitches at your writing group win."

"I wouldn't call them that," she protested.

"They're only so critical because they're jealous of your talent. I believe in you." He unscrewed the cap on a bottle of wine. "Get your laptop. Please? Pretty please?"

He angled his head with that hopeful smile Olivia couldn't resist.

"All right." She fetched the laptop from the sitting room. That reminded her she hadn't been able to back today's writing up to the cloud. "The broadband's out. Hopefully the router just needs resetting. Where is it?"

Jacob was slicing chicken breasts for a stir-fry. He paused, holding the sharp knife in the air. "Oh, damn. That must be why they were digging up the road just past the junction."

"Oh." Olivia didn't know what else to say to that.

"They'll have it fixed as soon as they can." He grinned at her, rueful. "That's life in the country, I'm afraid. We'll just have to make our own entertainment."

The wicked promise in his intense eyes and the slow curve of his lips sent a sensuous thrill through her.

Jacob started chopping an onion. "Read me what you've been working on today, and don't forget your wine."

Olivia still wasn't keen, but she did her best. Reading out what she had written showed her where she'd repeated herself, and which clunky sentences needed reworking. Jacob had plenty of suggestions, but she didn't necessarily agree with him. Not that she said so. All told, Olivia was relieved when dinner was ready and she could close the laptop. They ate, and then they took the rest of the wine upstairs where he entertained her very thoroughly indeed.

The next day, she lazed in bed while Jacob got up and showered. He kissed her quickly before he left.

"I'll lock the front door behind me, so you'll feel safe. I'll pick up a curry on my way home."

"That'll be lovely, thank you." As he left the bedroom, Olivia sat up quickly. "Jacob? When you get to the office, can you find out when the broadband will be sorted?"

He didn't answer, already hurrying down the creaking stairs. He must not have heard her. Never mind.

She got up, showered and dressed, and headed downstairs for breakfast. She was just going into the sitting room when she heard a thud in the study, just the same as the day before.

Going into the study, Olivia found a hefty tome on the floorboards in front of the bookcase. A Victorian history of the county, bound in red leather stamped with gold lettering, had landed with its pages splayed, open at a list of notable events in 1455.

On the 1st of November, which the book helpfully explained was All Saints' Day, Rosamund Guy had met her fiancé, Neville Randall, in Irby Woods. They were never seen again. Suspicions arose that Neville had murdered Rosamund and fled. Years later, a woman's bones were discovered buried among the roots of a tree. The tree had the intertwined initials

RG and NR carved into its bark. Her family swore her ghost walked the woods, unable to rest until her killer was hunted down and brought to justice.

Olivia checked the map in the front of the book. Irby wasn't that far from Bradley. Did every thicket in this county shelter a ghost with a ghastly tale of domestic violence? She put the book back on the shelf and went to make the most of another uninterrupted day to write.

When she heard Jacob's key in the lock that evening, she was ready to explain why she didn't really want to read him her day's work tonight. She didn't have to. He had a fragrant takeaway bag in one hand and a DVD boxset in the other.

"I thought we'd go old-school this evening." He'd got hold of Season One of *The West Wing* from somewhere.

Olivia laughed. 'Why not?'

She heard the front door close behind Jacob the next morning, and remembered she'd again forgotten to ask him if he knew when they'd have Internet access.

As she ate her breakfast, Olivia grew more irritated. For all she knew, the broadband problem had already been sorted. It couldn't be that hard to find the router, reset it, and find out.

She finished her toast and went outside. Walking slowly around the farmhouse, she looked for the point where the cable went into the wall. It was under the study window, hidden behind some flourishing hydrangeas. Olivia went inside and realised the wire must come into the alcove beside the fireplace – only a door from floor to ceiling had turned that into a cupboard, and it was locked. She searched the desk drawers for the key, but they were empty. Not even a pencil or a Post-It pad to write herself a reminder to ask Jacob to reset the router that evening. He must have the key.

She jumped as a book hit the floor behind her. Seriously? She turned and scowled at the shelves before she picked up the dour black volume. *Notable County Trials*. Olivia wrinkled her nose as she read the grim page where the book had fallen open. In 1805, Tom Otter had travelled from Nottinghamshire to work as a navvy in Lincoln. He seduced Mary Kirkham who soon became pregnant. Tom was forced to wed Mary, and the parish authorities insisted he paid something called a bastardy bond, to provide for the child's upkeep until it was old enough to be apprenticed.

But Tom Otter was already married. He'd abandoned a wife and child in his home village. Whether he was afraid his bigamy would be discovered, or for some other reason, Otter persuaded Mary to go away with him. Perhaps he told her they were going to start a new life in Nottinghamshire. Whatever he had said, her body was found near Saxilby and taken to the village's Sun Inn.

Olivia scanned the rest of the entry. Tom Otter had been convicted and hanged. Presumably that meant one less ghost wandering Lincolnshire in search of justice. She went to place the book back on the shelf, but changed her mind and put it on the desk instead.

Why were the books falling onto the floor? Each one was a different size, and belonged on a different shelf. Olivia racked her brains. Mice? She didn't think that was likely, but she couldn't exactly google for better ideas. She emptied the bookcase, stacking everything on the desk, looking for some sort of clue. Nothing. Certainly nothing as obvious as a nibbled hole.

Thoughtful, Olivia put the books back and went into the kitchen to wash her grimy hands. Jacob kept the house wonderfully clean and tidy, but books always held dust. She looked under the sink. Maybe there would be mouse traps she could set. As long as they were humane ones. All she found were basic cleaning supplies.

Olivia took a coffee into the sitting room. She tried to start her next chapter, but she couldn't concentrate, so she decided to look over what she had already written that week. Her favourite creative writing podcasts stressed the importance of authors revising their own work. That didn't go quite how she expected. By lunchtime, when she checked her software's metrics, her word total for the week was down by nearly a quarter.

Olivia gave up, and spent the afternoon reading some of the books of local folklore from the bookcase in the study. To her guilty relief, Jacob didn't ask how she had got on when he got back from work that evening.

As he cooked fillet steak and crushed new potatoes with garlic-dressed broccoli, he was full of ideas for taking a trip abroad later in the year. They could go to Greece, or maybe

Spain. Had Olivia ever thought about Tunisia? What about a real adventure, somewhere long-haul? Indonesia maybe, or why not Australia? As he held her hand across the table, and topped up her glass with red wine, Olivia smiled and nodded and let him talk.

Mostly, she was thinking it would be nice to get home to her own flat in Birmingham. They had planned to go back on Sunday, but Olivia decided she wanted to leave a day sooner. She'd find some way to tell Jacob tomorrow.

The next morning, Jacob left for work. Olivia had her breakfast, and yes, she heard another thud in the study, just as was just about to have another look for that cupboard key. She threw open the door and saw a small squat figure by the bookcase. It had its back to her, and it was about as tall as a toddler. Bare-legged and bare-armed, its long pale hair flowed down to its knees, obscuring its ragged clothes. The scent of woodlands and grassy paths filled the room.

"What the—?"

The creature spun around, and stared up at her, startled. A moment later, an exasperated scowl creased its wizened, bearded face. It was a boggart, Olivia realised. She had been reading about them just the day before. She hadn't believed they were real, obviously. But this creature was standing right here in front of her.

The boggart grunted, irritated. It turned around and picked up the book it had just dropped. Lifting the heavy volume high over its head, the creature slammed it down on the floorboards a second time, staring at her, unblinking. It stamped a bare, brown foot with unmistakable emphasis, and then it simply disappeared.

Going over to the desk, Olivia landed heavily in the chair. A boggart? Seriously? But the damp, green smell lingered. She had heard the thud of the book hitting the floor. The leatherbound volume still lay there with its pages spread open. She wasn't imagining any of that.

What was the creature doing here? From the stories she'd read, some boggarts were tricky and treacherous, but others wanted to help... Olivia sprang up and snatched the book off the floor. She swallowed hard as she read the story the boggart had for her today.

Bessie was a farmer's daughter and her sweetheart's name was Fox. He swore his everlasting devotion, and they arranged to meet one night in the woods. To run away together? The storyteller didn't say. The night before, though, Bessie woke from an unnerving dream. The storyteller didn't share that either, but Bessie went to meet her lover early enough to hide up in a tree. She waited to see what Fox might do when he arrived.

He turned up with a shovel. Bessie watched him dig a grave. When that was done, he sat down to wait for her to come. Bessie clung to the tree, staying as still as she possibly could. Eventually, Fox wearied of waiting. He grabbed his shovel, scraped the earth back into the grave, and headed home.

Bessie stayed in the tree, heartsick, trembling so hard that the leaves on the branches shook. When she was certain that Fox had gone, she climbed down and hurried home. The following day, Fox came to call, professing his love and asking why she had let him down. But Bessie had confessed all to her father. The farmer had seen the freshly dug grave for himself. He and his men seized Fox and dragged the villain off to prison.

Olivia's hands shook so violently that the page blurred. Her mouth was dry and her heart was racing. She dropped the old book on the desk and looked around for the boggart. There was no sign of the creature. She closed her eyes and ran her hands through her hair, trying to make sense of this insanity.

She clenched her fists and gripped her hair so hard that her scalp hurt. The pain was real. She wasn't asleep. This wasn't a dream. She wasn't imagining the boggart, incredible though that might seem. What had she imagined about Jacob, though? What fairy stories had he told her? What was he planning to do with her next? What did the boggart know?

Olivia moved fast. Running through to the kitchen, she opened the back door and searched every inch of the gardens, front and back. At least she didn't find any freshly dug earth. That was some consolation. Some, not much.

Back in the house, she raced upstairs, two steps at a time. She threw her clothes and everything else into her suitcase and took it down to the hall. Next, she searched the kitchen for something she could use to break into that cupboard. Get the broadband working, and she could book a taxi. If she couldn't get online? She'd damn well walk until she found another house or got a phone signal. She had to get out of here before Jacob came back from work.

Olivia took a carving knife and a sharpening steel into the study. She looked at the door between the fireplace and the wall. Was it a cupboard? What if she opened it and found some stairs? Did this house have a cellar? Was there some gruesome Bluebeard's chamber below the farmhouse? How many women had Jacob brought here before her? How many of them had left?

"Sister Anne, Sister Anne," Olivia muttered under her breath. She wished she had someone to ask for advice.

Sharp knocking shattered the silence. Olivia yelped and dropped the knife and the steel. The boggart tsked loudly with exasperation. She saw it was crouching on top of the bookcase, barely able to fit in the tight gap beneath the ceiling.

Olivia bit her lip. "I'm sorry. You startled me."

The boggart waved that away. Then it jabbed a thick yellow fingernail down towards its feet.

"What?" Olivia dragged the desk chair over to the bookcase and climbed up so she could see. The boggart retreated as far as it could.

"That's the key?" She looked at the creature with desperate hope. "For the cupboard?"

The boggart folded its withered arms. Its sardonic look asked her what else it could be. Then it vanished again.

Olivia grabbed the key and got off the chair. The lock opened smoothly and the door didn't lead into some nightmare. The cupboard was empty apart from the router and three things on the shelf below. Olivia switched the router on. While lights pulsed with its start-up routine, she opened the flimsy plastic ring-binder and read the first laminated page.

'Welcome to West Buslingthorpe Farm. We're delighted to

welcome you to our family home…'

She turned pages listing bin days and the local recycling rules, emergency contact numbers and recommendations for shops in Market Rasen.

"This is a sodding AirBnB!" Olivia glanced at the boggart who had reappeared to sit on the edge of the desk, swinging its bare feet. It looked quizzically at her.

Besides the folder, she found a computer tablet in a black leather case and a large brown paper envelope. The envelope held a Do It Yourself Will form that had been filled in. Apparently, Olivia was revoking all previous wills and testaments and leaving her entire estate to Jacob. How the hell had he learned to copy her handwriting so well? Her forged signature was perfect. All the thing needed was witness signatures and a date.

She threw the fake will onto the desk and opened the tablet. Pressing the power button showed her it was still half-charged. The screen demanded a pass code.

A surge of emotions caught her unawares. Humiliation. Disappointment. Fear. She choked on a sob and tossed the tablet onto the desk. Slumping into the chair, she buried her face in her hands.

The boggart started knocking again, demanding her attention. It was on the windowsill now. Seeing her looking its way, the creature leaned forward to breathe on the leaded pane. It wrote four numbers on the clouded glass: 9713.

Olivia wiped away tears with a frantic hand. "That's the code? For this?"

She didn't wait for the boggart's nod before she tried it. The code worked. Checking the My Files icon showed her a list of numbered folders with her name. The first one was photographs of pages from her bullet journal. So that's how he'd learned to forge her handwriting. Screenshots showed posts from her social media. So that's how Jacob knew about her hobbies, and the films and books that she liked.

Another file of PDFs showed Olivia a whole lot more. Jacob had downloaded Grandad's obituary from the *Birmingham Mail*. That told the story of the family engineering firm his own father had founded. How the company had grown now into a thriving enterprise with four factories manufacturing hi-tech components for the car industry. How this was still a family business, with her parents and uncles and aunts in senior management, while Olivia and her cousins started on the shop floor. There was a copy of the Rightmove listing when Gran downsized from the seven-bedroom house in Solihull. Jacob had even somehow got hold of scans of Olivia's grandfather's will. He knew exactly how much money she had inherited.

No wonder he fancied going to Australia. Olivia's blood ran cold. Would she have come home from that trip, or would she have died in some tragic 'accident'? Then Jacob would produce that fake will...

She felt oddly calm as she photographed the envelope and its contents with her phone. She took pictures of the holiday rental folder too. Then she put everything back in the cupboard.

"If I take anything away, he'll know that I know," she

explained to the curious boggart. "We don't want anything tipping him off, or he'll disappear before he's arrested. Let's hope the police do one of those dawn raids and smash in his front door," she added savagely.

The boggart shrugged. Olivia picked up the tablet, the carving knife and the sharpening steel. "Come on."

The boggart vanished, reappearing next to the fireplace when she walked into the sitting room. Olivia opened up her laptop and searched the bag for the right cable.

"Obviously he's been stalking me, and planning some sort of fraud, but I don't know exactly what laws he's broken. Cait will," she said with satisfaction, as she connected the tablet to her laptop. "She's a solicitor."

She had no idea if the boggart understood her, but maybe her tone was enough. Either way, the little creature beamed at her. Olivia started copying Jacob's files. Not only the ones labelled with her name. Either he'd targeted other women in the past, or he was researching future victims. No wonder he kept this tablet locked away where he thought no one could find it.

"I was stupidly slow to see what those stories were telling me," she said ruefully to the boggart. "I'm glad you didn't give up."

The boggart tilted its head one way and then the other, indicating surprisingly effectively that yes, she had been tiresomely dense, and no, it didn't hold that against her.

"I can't—" Olivia broke off, remembering those stories where thanking boggarts didn't turn out well. How could she show her appreciation? What did the creatures want in those tales? "If you like milk… have you ever had ice cream?"

The boggart's raised brows and pursed lips suggested it hadn't, but was willing to try.

Olivia left her laptop gathering evidence and went into the kitchen. She was right. There was a two-litre tub of Cornish dairy vanilla untouched in the freezer. She pulled off the lid and placed the ice cream in the middle of the floor. Putting the carving knife and steel away, she found a silicon spoon which she stuck into the ice cream.

"Be careful, it's cold." She left the boggart capering with glee as it contemplated the feast to come.

Back in the sitting room, she felt apprehensive again. As soon as the files were downloaded, she emailed everything to Caitlin with a promise to explain what was going on as soon as she got home. Now she needed to leave as fast as she could. Her hands shook as she packed away her laptop, and used her phone to contact a local taxi firm.

"I need a ride from West Buslingthorpe Farm to the nearest railway station, as quickly as possible, please."

She struggled to keep her voice level, but the dispatcher didn't seem to notice.

"A car will be with you inside half an hour."

"Thank you." Olivia ended the call and heaved a shuddering sigh.

She put the tablet back on the shelf and switched off the router. She locked the cupboard and put the key back on top of the bookcase. Locking the front door, she posted the house key through the letter box and waited in the porch with her coat, laptop and suitcase.

The taxi arrived twenty minutes later. As the friendly driver drove away down the lane, Olivia slumped on the back seat, limp with relief. She had escaped this unexpected nightmare. Once she was on a train, she felt safer. As the miles passed, she started thinking ahead. First thing tomorrow, she and Cait would go to the police. She would block Jacob on her phone, on her socials, on her email, however he tried to contact her, and she'd get a restraining order. Hell, if she had to, she'd hire a bodyguard.

A bit later, something else occurred to Olivia as she stared out of the train window. Her podcasts often discussed drawing on your own life for inspiration. She could use this horrible experience to write a much better novel than that family saga.

Though she decided she wouldn't mention the boggart to her creative writing group.

Author Comment

I first encountered Lincolnshire's rich heritage of local legends when I started primary school in the village of Waddington in 1969. In my memory, the school library had books of history, folklore, and fantasy stories imagined by writers like Alan Garner shelved side by side. Whether or not that recollection is accurate, I grew up with factual books, traditional fiction, and original stories, as related and interwoven elements in my reading. In my career as a novelist, I have learned how grounding a story with touches of reality gives readers the firm footing they need to take the next step into the truly fantastic.

I vividly recall finding Yallery Brown terrifying as a small child. I seem to remember not leaving the garden for weeks, not about to risk encountering him myself. Being scared didn't mean I wasn't intrigued, though. Could there really be a whole hidden world of creatures watching me which I couldn't see? Stories about boggarts and their kin have caught my attention ever since. I've found them fascinating, seeing how varied these creatures can be, and how their motives and desires are always entirely their own. This has influenced my current contemporary fantasy series of novels, starting with *The Green Man's Heir*.

Of course, as I grew up, I learned that keeping children safe is a central function of folklore. Other stories offer different warnings, especially to young girls. A great deal has changed through the centuries, but darker aspects of human nature have not. Being invited to contribute to this anthology renewed my acquaintance with Lincolnshire's boggarts, and I decided to explore the ways such an ageless observer could use traditional tales to alert a modern young woman to the dangers of wishful thinking, and of deliberate deceit.

GRIM GOES FISHING

FROM A NEW LAY OF HAVELOK THE DANE

Rahul Gupta

'...it will not be amisse, to say something concerning yᵉ Common tradition of her first founder *Grime*, as yᵉ inhabitants name him. The tradition is thus. *Grime*, a poore Fisherman, as he was launching into yᵉ Riuer for fish in his little boate vpon *Humber*, espyed not far from him another boate, empty (as he might conceaue) which by yᵉ fauour of yᵉ wynde & tyde still approached nearer & nearer vnto him. He meetes itt, wherein he founde onely a Childe wrapt in swathing clothes, purposely exposed (as it should seeme) to yᵉ pittylesse rage of yᵉ wilde & wide Ocean. He, moued with pitty, takes itt home, & like a good foster-father carefully nourisht itt in his owne occupation: but yᵉ childe contrarily was wholy deuoted to exercises of martiall sports, & at length by his signall valour obteyned such renowne, that he married yᵉ King of England's daughter, & last of all founde who was his true Father, & that he was Sonne to yᵉ King of *Denmarke*; & that *Haueloke* (for such was his name) exceedingly aduanced & enriched his foster-father *Grime*, who thus enriched, builded a fayre Towne neare the place where *Haueloke* was founde, & named it *Grimesby*. That *Haueloke* did sometymes reside in *Grimesby*, may be gathered from a great

189

blew Boundry-stone, lying at yᵉ East ende of *Briggowgate*,
which retaines yᵉ name of *Haueloke's-Stone* to this day. Agayne
yᵉ great priuiledges & immunityes, that this Towne hath in
Denmarke above any other in England (as freedome from Toll,
& yᵉ rest) may fairely induce a Beleife, that some preceding
fauour, or good turne called on this remuneration…'

    —Gervase Holles, MP, Mayor of Grimsby 1636 &c., MS. Harl. 6829.

Blind night-abyss. Black tides rising
wash and welter. Wind-tang a smart
reek raw with brack. Rumour of surf-
upheavals' eddy in-draws its moan.
Saltbillows seethe. The sands whisper.
Work of waters.
                The waves cresting
dive downsunken. Deep wellings climb.
Groundswell's regurge grinds trawled shingle.
Its sway an aura, Sea wields the shock
of its brunt being; and its bulk that mass
endlessly other, forever moving
astir unstanched. The streaming flux
writhes restlessly; the rough element's
throes thrive to warp throngs of changeling
forms phantomlike: floodwaters spawn
bodies born flotsamed; their blurred guises
merge manyshapen, then melt drowning
in the void vortex —as their voices call
to a brink brimming. Brine-gush lathers,

chafes chesil-pebbles, churns to breakers'
spindrifted spume; the spray-drizzle
stings staiths ashore.

                    Storm is gathering.

From Ægir's eelbilge to Ymir's crown,
heavenroads of hawks: in the helm of the sky
—Blue-One's brainpan that burdens dwarves—
murk is mounting; Moon's bridlepath
is gloom-shrouded. Gust-flurries awhirl:
housed high above seas in hidden eyries,
the weavers of winds waft nightshadow's
veils of vapour. It devours twilight;
swirls swoop over and swallow the stars,
glide grimplumaged; groping wingspans
fan out the fume: a frown of darkness.
Pitchblack it prowls; a pall thrumming
with glowers and growls; glints that smoulder.
   Thunders throne him: Thor's juggernaut
rolls full-career; he is riding the winds,
steers the tempest in his storm-chariot,
pilots cyclones. He plies the swinge:
the goat-goader giddies-up fiercely;
spoked axle-spins spurn floors of cloud
—whiplash whistles— his whickering pair,
Toothgrinder, Toothgnasher, his team of goats,
bite their bridles, their bleats snorting.
Drum dinning hooves; he drives them hard;

the rims rumble on the roof of the sky.
Black bands like smoke boil in spirals,
writhe around him, as he rallies his hosts,
the weathers enthralled to the thunder-weapon:
brow-moons ablaze, the bane of ogres,
the wagon-driver who wields Mjœlnir
the oak-striker, with his iron gauntlets
clasps its handle that crackles with zigzags,
heaves high and aims the hammer of the lightning.

The cloud-arrows, cruelly volleyed
rainbodkins rake the rearing flanks
of the brine-whelmings, on the blast of a gale
from the icy East with an edge like a chisel.
Rumpus mutters; rock-slidelike snarls
stammer, are stifled: then with stutters and cracks
the bang throbbing from the thunder-burst
shakes main and shore with a shuddering boom.
Launched lightningbolts lash the ocean,
forked flicker-barbs. As fleet glimpses
dreampictures dazzle in the darts of levin:
walls of water; waves surge in peaks,
horns honed by wind, heaving ridges
flash, ravenflint; floodwaters swell;
Spearman's expanse: spate churning froth.
The whistling squall whips the currents up;
streams strive aloft: storm beats downward,
tall tides rampant entangle with clouds,

rollers roiling; horizons drowned
obscure borders of Sky and Earth
—the ocean-walled urn of tempests;
the gale-enwreathed garth of mortals.

   Whalemere howling with hungry growls
the waters teem with worm-kindreds;
the mere-monsters' mood is whetted:
seldcouth seadragons, scenting carnage,
floodpower-fathomed, flounder dredging
wide wavebedrock and wade to shore;
garfish gambol in their greed for prey;
knuckerholes gnawing.

                   North musters sleet,
hard hailshowers' harvestless grain;
kernels coldest.

               Then those keel-riding
harbour-horses on the whales' acre
—fish feeding-grounds— must fear for their lives,
when tempest towers at the tossing prow;
spume-sprayed the hull spins steerboardless,
the bulwarks swamped by brack-welter,
the mare of the mere's mast-yards topple,
clinkered lapstrakes crack and splinter:
brineguests must bathe —abandon ship
and fail to breathe the fishes' air
—jump jetsamed in giant's-woundthawing;
beersmith's-yeastsurf; abyss of eels;
the gannets' larder: the engulfing chasms'

ill-eddying swirl. That ale they quaff
bitter bloatswillage brewed by Ægir:
dark frothy dregs; their drowned bodies
trapped entangled in the trawling nets
Rán reels under, roaring Ægir's
brinecold bedmate.
                                    Bloodshot the foam
at rock-skerries rife with lobsters;
water weaponful: wide-gaping jaws
bare battletushes; a broil of spines,
fangteeth and fins. Flood bloodied scuds.
Rich pickings rise in ruddled slurry.
They flock to the feast: fulmar and tern,
for orts and offal; the ernes stooping
with whetted beaks, white-tailed eagles
delve deep their talons, dewy-pinioned;
swart-sallowbrown, the swan of wounds,
hazy-plumaged; the horn-nebbed one.
Scream of scavengers. Scolding jargons
chide, rame and chirm as they choose morsels;
the squabbling skua, the skirl of whaup,
grey herring-gulls' gabble and yammer:
mews' glee at meat.
                                    Morrow-tide weakly
leavens the darkness, and lulls the storm.
High heavencandle is huddled in cloud.
    Then come up to the reefs Rán and Ægir's
ninefold nestlings, knotter of meshes'

billows-daughters, to bleach their hair.
Spools shrugged into spume in spilling hanks
of rippling ringlets reach through the waves:
flax flosses out fronds and tendrils,
the curls coiling to cove and wharf;
tress-tentacles tickle all the coasts
and dishevel ashore.
                    A shifting firth;
an arm of the sea.
                  East wind dropping,
the heaving surges hush to stillness;
the surf-struggle sinks abating.
The walls of land that weathered tempests,
staiths stormbeaten, stayed the onslaught.
Meretowers melt.
                  Mews are wailing.
In wide heavens winds veer and yawn.
Sweeping breakers swirl back foaming.
Shoals grind the shelves of a shingle bay
where a grey river greets the ocean.

Amid the frost-phantoms of a foggy dawn
Grim goes to work, at the gloomy hour
of livid twilight: leaves his homestead,
threads through the dunes' thigh-high tussocks,
saltmarsh, siltdyke; in silence till
the fisherman flushes the fowl nesting
from rush-reedbeds, redshank and snipe;

lagoon-grottoes' gluts of lamprey,
samphire-dingles —a salt presence
gropes goosepimpling with a gruesome allure—
winds wide mudflats; wades down to the shore's
kingdom of kelp. Cold grey as flint
the horizon rims a rink of slate.
A withering wind; wolf-tooth-bitter.
Marine redolence of rancid weed.
Breakers' thunder. Brute threat of sky
and with a loom, the sea.
                    The long combers
wash the beaches; waves arch their necks;
race rolling back, and rear again;
prance pawing hooves, their pluming manes
froth faxwaxen; fetlocked with spume,
nostrils neezing, with noise of onrush,
lapping, lathered, the leaping steeds,
ply over ply, are pool-folded.
Above the white horses wheel mews shrieking;
alderman eyes augury-birds'
gliding gaggles; they graze in mobs;
their skeins pucker, then scatter aside,
spin spiralling, and speed away.
   All eddymingled, the eagre-streams;
Barbwielder's bath blends its settlings.
Strewn over the strand, storm has broadcast
Ocean's harvest, the after-math
of wrack and wreckage, careened in ooze:

dulse-hung driftwood; in dimpled ruts
bladderwrack blackens. Barnacled spars
lulled lopsided in lakes of slime;
oak earls have taught the art of swimming
surf tumbles and sifts, and salt scorches;
goods for salvage, the gear of the drowned;
ribs wrenched from hulks; rags of sailcloth,
lanyard-belayed amid the lobster-creels:
idle awnings.
                    Their eyes on stalks,
crabs creep sideways, clacking pincers.
Lugworms uplift little sandcastles.

Yet there at the sandbar is the sound-plying
tidegoer tamed by tether-cables:
his ocean-otter, anchorbond-fast,
stays for her steersman, her stem bridling;
rocked at roadstead by the rising swell.
Gulfcunning Grim at the grey margin
hauls out of hithe, and heaves to launch
the clinkered coble —the currents grinding
shell on shingle; shore-defying
brawn shoves abeam— the beast of the slipway
runs her keelstrake into rushing surf.
The prow plunges; planks are bucking;
he climbs aboard, casts off moorings
to ride the rollers.
                    As he rows he sees

fleet-floating ones on furrowed ripples
bathe breastfeathers in the brown gullies
of the swans' sailroad: the swimming fowl,
preening pinions with piping cries.
Above the floods' darkness the frowning sky
lours leadenclouded, a ledge of grey
in piled layers, its pending roof
stretched stonemantled upon steely waters;
ironhued to the eye, edged with lustre
at the wan weathergleam, windowed eastward:
bleak beams glaring, bleared and sallow.

    Then once the masttree's mere-arraying
sail's cinctured tight, sea-stays are braced
—cordage creaking— and clews are trimmed,
the bunt bellies in a breeze astern:
the prow perking, pilot thirsty
for Ægir's ale. Underway the craft
drives deep water. Drenched with spindrift
rein-rigging hums. He rides his steed
of the track of gulls: the tarred wader's
keel is cutting, the cold fathoms
burst brine-surges on braided strakes,
well-clinkered wands of the wake-carver.
Mind on mereflood —mews reel aside—
the coxswain cuddles the kicking tiller.

    She wafts then on wavehome at winds' urging,
floats foamybosomed, flying birdlike,
the tide-treader; timbers dinning,

the surfwood soars the sound-channels,
crest-glider's cruise; until her keel pierces
open Ocean: Ymir's bloodstream
fosters foison of folk with scales,
haddock and hakes' harvest-acres,
redfishes realm, ruled by mackerel,
saithes' seafastness.

                    With song-magic
Ránlover's runes enrapture air
to raise the wraiths of roke-vapour
and foam-frettings, as frosted puffs
blow burred by cold to blooms of steam;
spun out of space, spider-gauzes
are fused fuscous, furring æther;
tissues toughen, teaselled to sheer
thistledown threads, the thatched weftage
clammy clusters of cloud-smother:
this hedge of hazes is the haar of that sea.
Its blankness blinds the bear-warrior;
fogbound in fume the fishing-boat
—waylaid by walls of wisps of smoke—
drifts in doldrums.

                    In the dewy hush,
with currents becalmed, chorus voices;
mist-muffled howls. The moan from the Odd
of Raven's-Ayre narrates to Grim
—whelps of whelmfloods whoop and gibber—
brother of Byleist and Bifrost-guard's

single combat for that sea-kidney
—amber amulet owed to Freyja,
the dwarves' trinket— a duel on the reefs,
gnomecorpse-Náinn's canoeshed-doors:
a jewel-jousting amid the giant's blood,
guised as selkies.
                              A gleam twinkles;
a shadow that shimmers shows through the fogs:
swart silhouette, swathed in dimness
yet the prow's profile plays glowing through,
as lighted taper the lantern-horn;
amid skeins scudding the skeleton hulls,
the mast falters, mainsail drooping;
she swings nearer on the sullen wallow.
Whorl-necked she hoves: a white, dazzling,
leeward-listing, longship of war.
He climbs the keel of that kings' galley.

None stands stationed at stern or beak.
Craft captainless. Uncrewed the thofts;
no hand to halyard; hulk gybes and yaws.
A dragon-dromond adrift on the tides.

Bulwark-bucklers, bright lindenshields
—preybird-painted— pegged still on racks;
grey gear in heaps. A ghost-vessel;
and this ship's shining in a shell of ice.

Lookouts won't ladder the lensed pinnacles.
The cold clenches, clustered on spars;
its freezing feathers fleece the stanchions:
mossed with moonbarbs; mirror-splinter grist.

As if tackled with ice. Timbered with ice.
Antlered with ice, this elk of the flood.
Ice on oarports. Ice-stark sailcloth
chimes on yardarms. Chill droplets have

eked icicles, the ooze frozen
to sparkling spikes spiral-twisted
like narwhal-horns; the knotting beasts
carved in keelposts, crystal-lacquered

frostbitten filigrees. Fossilized in glaze,
its rind renders the rig's cordage,
shrouds encrusted, and sheets to bony
wires of silver: winter cobwebs.

Iron ice shackles her oak planking;
hoary harness to helmet ships.
The frost-fetters flicker gemstones
rainbowed with rime. A rapt silence.

Foot-falls' clangour —frore mists of breath—
keel-climbing Grim is crossing thwarts.
The eastern airt opened with glades

of culver-colour and coral blushes,
mists are moving. Murk is fading.

    Beneath the awning a nestled bundle
cries out and kicks the clouts aside:
a baby boy in the bosom of a longship.
Grim views in gold, on the gold swaddlings,
serpent-symbols; silken vestments;
rune-written torque wrapped in sendal;
the waif is wound in a war-banner,
gonfanon-garbed in the gold samite,
ancient oriflamme of Ingvi's Folk:
a royal heirloom to robe a babe in
from some tribe's treasury, travel beside him,
into the floodtides' might —far departing
cradle rocking on the cold waters—
a boon from whoever embarqued this infant
from a forlorn seashore, launched him drifting
across the currents —castaway child—
with that banner to bless him.

                    The boarder sees

his fair features; fiercely piercing
ice-bright his eyes, of eagle keenness;
on Grim's finger his grip is strong.

    It is then that the sunlight sears through the fogs.
Heatwending high the heaven-candle
climbs clear of wrack and cloud-tatters:
the sea-farer's circling promise;
enemy of ice. Egg-field dwellers,

mews, mount the air: the massed seafowls'
whiteplumaged hosts whirl and cackle,
the gulls gathering to greet with clamour
the bright beacon. Her burning rays
melt mist and fume. Murk is vanquished,
the welkin-wanness, by the weather-jewel.
Lightwonder laughs as lurking dusk,
narrow shades of night, the numb wintry
dark's downfallen, as dawn rises
—Old Ægir smiles endless dimples—
on a Yule morning with the youthful sun.
At their topmost tower, two messengers
in wide-pinioned wind-riding flight,
hover high aloft: they hail with trills,
glide down and gaze with golden eyes,
and soar circling; then sweep away
—errand-eagles— to the elf-roundel.

Thus as west Wáda voyaged, the pilot of Wingelote,
cleaving the cold waters, giant king of the Helsings
—nor was it neap on the whaleroad, but a depth of nine ells when
he bore from the brine Wéland, a child on brawny shoulders—
as Sheave on his shield-cradle washed ashore on Angeln;
as from Finn Folkwalding's hall, avenging feud with slaughter,
the hero Hengest was driven to Kent and hungered for land;
from the east as Ingvi the Lord crossed in his ocean-chariot
from Fródi's fruitful kingdom —where drudging frost-giant girls
heaved at Hamlet's millstone, turned the harsh axle-tree;

the tides from their turning changed to the briny taste of weeping:
fettered there the frost-maidens turned that Fródi throneless—
so to Humber's haven Havelok the Dane,
a freight salvaged by Father Grim,
was wafted to Lindsey, on wings of storm,
to our folk-founder, to this fisher-town,
our anchorage, from over the waves,
the swans' sealanes, seeking England:
thrower of menhirs; the throne-claimer.

Author Comment

An underlying concept is that of composing a quasi-translation of the poetry for Grim and Havelok which should exist but doesn't. I do *not* however aim to finish with some kind of forgery of a mediæval poem. I strive to push further than that, with many personal modern touches that were not practised by, or were impossible for, the mediæval poets. My work is profoundly traditionalist, faithfully dovetailed with extant sources, but traditionalism does embrace innovation and development from within the traditions – with, I hope, authenticity and subtlety.

Growing up in the Lincolnshire Wolds, my parents worked in Grimsby. I was in town throughout my youth, a regular at the Library, where, having passed the effigies of Grim and Havelok from the thirteenth-century Great Town Seal, I would while away hours poring over the *Oxford English Dictionary* or the *Encyclopædia Britannica*, ensconced in Reference on the top floor. In Children's, downstairs, I read illustrated versions of *Beowulf*, the Vǫlsungs, retellings from The Eddas. We passed the statue of Grim carrying Havelok out of the sea on his shoulders every time we drove home. The poem *Havelok the Dane* became something like a civic ode to my birth-town, in tribute, celebrating her Anglo-Scandinavian heritage, which felt as if it were my own culture even as a child.

Form and content should present an aesthetic unity. The versification is so-called alliterative (syllabic, quantitative, and accentual) verse. This was an oral-formulaic art performed by traditional makars: poetry as sound addressed by voice to ear. I have used the Old English form including the hypermetric variation, and the closely-akin Old Norse *fornyrðislag*, "Old Story-Mode". The diction is likewise meant to be a blend of kindred Old English and Norse traditions, weaving a style suited to the subject: the setting is the Humber Estuary in a legendary Danelaw of a fictional 800 AD.

THE RIVER RAT

Nick Triplow

There was something quietly heroic about Gilo Sweeney's arrival on the morning of Jack Causey's funeral, not that he saw it that way. He stepped off the early bus, taking in the smoke rising from chimneys on Waterside Road. There was ice in the wind as he walked the straight half mile towards the river. He shrugged deeper into his overcoat. This was how he'd remembered it, the town perpetually on the edge of winter.

The gates of Trathen's boatyard were chained and padlocked. Patrick was nowhere to be seen, though he was usually at work by eight o'clock. A gust of wind clattered the corrugated iron roof on the repair shed. A tarpaulin flapped loose from the boat it was meant to be protecting. Jack used to say you could catch a whiff of Stockholm tar in the breeze at the northern end of Waterside, a ghost smell of ropes from the old days of the ropery, the boatyard and river traffic. That morning, it had the air of a deserted shanty town as he crossed the haven bridge for a view over the water. A dozen or so small boats settled at their moorings in the mud. He felt a pang of recognition at Jack Causey's tidy little cabin cruiser, *Marianne*, still tied up at the jetty, but was more interested in the grime-covered houseboat moored high on the bank, an optimistic 'for sale' sign in the wheelhouse window. The nameless tug had served as his and Patrick's bolthole. Patrick's when he was too drunk to go home and face Lorna, Gilo's on the night Kev Causey had called him a worthless river rat and threatened to kill him if he showed his face in town again.

In Patrick's absence, he toyed with the idea of walking to the traveller camp on the outskirts of town to see Gran May, but it wasn't a visit he could afford to rush and would be better made after he'd done what he came to do. He sat by the boatyard and looked across the Humber. Karen had packed him up with bread rolls and cheese left over in the kitchen before he left Bristol on Tuesday night. She said they'd manage a day or two in his absence, but he was expected back for the weekend. He ate a rough sandwich and waited by the river for as long as he dared.

Tasha Causey saw him first. She was standing with mourners on the grass verge outside the family home, holding hands with a little girl in a blue coat, Kev and Sean Causey and Des Birch close by. Des caught Gilo's eye. His face hardened. The next Gilo knew, Kev Causey was striding out, suit jacket flapping open, belly busting at his shirt buttons.

"The fuck you doing here, Sweeney?"

Gilo unshouldered his bag, freeing his hands. "I'm sorry about your dad, Kev."

"Fuck off."

"I'm here for the funeral, then I'm leaving. No trouble."

"You heard me, pikey rat."

Gilo swallowed the insult. "I came to pay my respects to Jack. That's all."

Kev took a step closer. Gilo stood his ground. Des Birch and

Sean Causey made the move to join them. Kev aching to make someone feel worse than he did; Des and Sean doing what they always did, picking up scraps. Hard to believe they'd grown up together, been mates. The hearse carrying Jack Causey turned the corner behind them. Gilo gestured as it slowed to a dignified halt. "Your dad's here, Kev."

Kev was speechless for a moment, the wind knocked out of him. Then he squared his shoulders and stuck a finger in Gilo's face. "Tick tock, pikey."

Two gloss-black Daimlers came to a stop behind the hearse. Causey sons and wives and kids bitched and bickered about who was to go in which car. Gilo heard Jack's voice in his head: *Look at that, boy. Not an ounce of sense between 'em. Pissing my money up the wall. Givin' it the big un and for what? They don't know the half of it, eh?*

Tasha tossed a glance in Gilo's direction as she helped the girl into the first car. Was that a flicker of regret? With Tasha, the look you thought heavy with one meaning might easily mean the opposite. She was probably curious to see what the years had done to him, whether he had it in him to give her brothers and her useless bloke a run for their money.

The cortege drove to the end of Waterside Road, past the new flats with their river view, the old coastguard cottage and the boatyard. Gilo turned his back and started walking. He sniffed the air, sensing something unpleasant coming his way. It wasn't tar in the breeze; it was blood.

You watch yerself, boy.

Gilo entered the church behind a dozen or so faces he recognised as Jack's former associates, none of whom recognised him. One – a detective sergeant from Grimsby – had taken a shine to Tasha some years back, then found himself in Jack's pocket. Gilo watched him casting an eye over the congregation as they shuffled into the few remaining spaces at the rear of the church. Jack's coffin was set at the altar. An elderly priest gave his blessing and invited them to kneel and pray. Whatever words they said, Gilo heard the prayers for what they truly meant: 'Bury him deep and protect us from his ghost.' The Jack he knew would have done his deal with the Devil by now. Gilo pictured him lifting his cap, scratching his nut and giving a look that said, *how 'bout you do this one for me and we'll call it even*. With Jack, there was no such thing as even. The Devil didn't stand a chance.

The service was cold and impersonal. Gilo struggled to hold a clear thought other than that he needed to leave the church and the town, to move far from its meanness and never return. But he sensed something else; there was a job Jack wanted him to finish. He came back to himself as the priest gave a final blessing. Kev, Sean and Des were joined by three other men he didn't know. They shouldered Jack's coffin through the main door and across the churchyard with the undertaker guiding them down uneven steps to the hearse. With Jack safely on board, Kev and Sean lit cigarettes. Des took the prime spot, front seat in the Daimler. Gilo came out with the crowd, stepping into the road to pass ditherers on the pavement. Tasha Causey reached out and drew him to one side. "Not so fast, stranger. You never said hello."

"Hiya Tash."

"You coming to the pub after?"

"That'd be popular."

"Come on, buy me a drink."

Des Birch's face appeared at the limo window. Gilo said, "You want to watch Kev make good on cutting me up or just trying to annoy Des?"

"Kev's got more than you to worry about. And I don't need to talk to you to get on Des's nerves. Too much Marmite on his toast and his day's ruined."

Des wound down the window. "Natasha Birch, we're going."

Gilo raised an eyebrow. "*Natasha Birch?*"

"He's making a point. See you in the pub, yeah?"

Des stepped out of the car, but stopped half way. "Get here, now."

"You'd best go," said Gilo.

"You'll come?"

"I'll think about it."

"It'll be worth your while." She pleaded with her eyes in spite of the grief between them. As if he'd never been away.

The cemetery was a 20-minute walk from the church, set on a shallow slope with a panoramic view over the river. As expected, this was a more select gathering of close family and friends – some dubious in Gilo's eyes. He made a mental note of who was in attendance, but kept his distance as the priest intoned earth, ashes and dust with the emotion of a Sunday afternoon takeaway order. Jack used to say there was nothing

Gilo didn't see. That afternoon he saw everything.

Truth was, Jack had the drop on the old men and their families who ran the town. He'd known who'd turn a blind eye for a favour, who'd respond better for the price of a large drink and who'd only take the hint with a kick in the bollocks round the back of Trathen's yard. Or in extreme cases, who they'd have to take for a ride upriver to Read's Island. Those times Jack called Gilo, no one else. Landing on Read's as darkness fell was often all it took. Give a man a shovel and tell him to dig his own grave, then let the bleakness and the cold and the thought of what might happen there play on his mind. They might decide to take a swing, but no one ever did. On an island in the river, there was nowhere to run. And now the old men and their families stood with the Causeys. It didn't feel right.

Gilo stood at Jack's graveside. Whatever needed taking care of, he was keeping quiet about it. Gilo hadn't made up his mind whether to join the Causeys at the pub. What did Tasha mean, *it'll be worth your while*? He was curious, he'd admit. But for the Causeys, blood ties would always come first. Forgetting that had been his first mistake all those years ago. Trusting Tasha about anything came a close second.

There were a dozen drinkers in The Black Swan. Empty plates, dry crusts and used serviettes told their own story. Gilo got the feeling the Causeys expected him sooner.

Des was at the bar. "Here he is, fresh from his master's

graveside. We saw yer." He went back to the table where the others were drinking.

Gilo bought a pint and stood at the bar to drink.

Tasha joined him. "You coming to sit down?"

"I said I'd drop by."

"Des said you were by the grave. He said it was like you were keeping guard."

"I was having a conversation."

"With Dad?"

He looked at her for the first time. "Why are you so desperate to get me involved? You think I'll find a way out for you and the girl?"

"Her name's Sara."

Gilo looked over at Sean, Kev, Des and the DS from Grimsby, pints lined up, talking, saying nothing. Des keeping his mouth shut for the most part. "He's in trouble, isn't he? Which means so are you. Kev as well, but he's too frightened to do anything about it in case he fucks up. Which he will."

"They want to talk to you."

"With or without Detective Sergeant Parkes in earshot?"

She was surprised he knew who Parkes was. Maybe they were hoping to pass him off as a distant cousin. He didn't get the chance to ask as a shout went up from the back of the bar, Jeanie Causey in a panic. Gilo turned in time to see Sean slide off the long seat, his head and torso slumped forward, legs splayed in front of him, colour drained from his face. Jeanie was on her feet screaming. Kev and Des looked on, unmoving. Parkes appeared amused by the whole thing. Tasha went to

Sean, knelt and felt for his pulse. She pressed her palm against his forehead, speaking softly all the time. Gilo pulled the table away and made space, then helped Tasha lay him down. He rolled up a coat and raised Sean's legs. Tasha gently pinched his forearm. "This used to happen when he was a kid. When things got too much for him, he'd shut down."

Gradually, a pinkness began to show in Sean's cheeks. He came round, muttering under his breath – something to do with a "broken engine" and "sand in the tank". He opened his eyes, looked from Tasha to Gilo, and said the word "boneyard."

Tasha said, "What about the boatyard?"

He shook his head and tried to lift himself up. Someone put a brandy in his hand.

Jeanie was hyperventilating in the corner.

"Get one for Jeanie, n'all," said Tasha.

Des and Kev helped Sean back to his seat. All smiles and pats on the back. *He'd had too much to drink too quickly. The day had taken it out of him. Laying down on the job as usual.* Kev's face told a different story; he was terrified.

Gilo made ready to leave. He picked up his rucksack.

Kev stood in his way. "Something you need to hear. Get yourself a drink and sit down."

Parkes rolled a ciggy and laid it in his baccy tin. "Family business. I'll leave you to it. I'm off out for a smoke."

Sean sipped brandy. Jeanie fretted. He told her he was fine and she should go home. Des wet his lips and loosened his tie, agonizing over the conversation they were about to have. It pained him, that much was obvious. Tasha joined them – she'd made arrangements for Sara to stay at a friend's house. Kev came back from the gents noticeably more confident than when he went in and took the vacant seat at the head of the table.

"I want what's on Read's Island. What you and me dad hid there."

Gilo glanced around the table. "Kev, I don't work for you. Remember?"

"But you worked for my dad and you know where he hid the important gear. I want it."

"What *gear*? And who says I'd risk ferrying fuck-all for you?" What did they think, Jack had stashed his life savings up there? Perhaps he shouldn't be surprised. For years the old man's stock response when asked what went on at Read's Island amounted to "Ask Gilo."

"You get us there and show us where he stashed it."

Gilo laughed. "Listen to yourself. Not a chance. Not for you, not for any of you."

Sean drummed his fingers on the table, timing his entry into the conversation.

Des chipped in first. "We can compensate you. You'll get your share. And if you wanted to come back to town – Kev?"

Gilo smiled to himself. "And why would I want to do that?"

Sean was determined to have his moment. "Gilo, look at it this way. Des is on the council. So's Martin Tilson and Robin Carr, friends of ours. Your family and your mate Patrick and his family live within the town boundary because the council allows them to park their caravans on our land. First thing we'll do is have them evicted and not in a nice way. No more home sweet home. We've got private security contractors ready to go at a day's notice. Second thing, the fire at the hotel last year – the place was gutted. You hear about that?"

Gilo had read the reports. The company that owned the hotel had gone into liquidation during the pandemic, though it had already looked like a dodgy proposition. He knew for a fact that Jack had been approached to invest and turned it down. The Fire Service investigators had called it arson from the off. It didn't take a genius to work out the rest.

"The hotel was a considerable investment for this town. That's right, Des. Yeah?"

Des swallowed hard, wishing Sean would shut up.

"Someone will go down for it. We've got a fair idea who, but a traveller with a grudge against the town and one of its more prominent families?"

And there it was, all Gilo needed to draw the threads together. Tasha knew which way the wind was blowing and wanted away from Des, maybe the town, too. Des had lost his investment in the hotel – probably not his own money – and was up to his neck in debt. Sean was desperate to carve out something for himself for the first time in his pointless life and Kev was intent on keeping the family business without his dad's instinct, influence and a basic grasp of how any of it worked. All of them wanting to know what he knew, as if the answers were buried on an uninhabited patch of land five miles upriver.

"Say I go to the island—"

"Me and Des are coming with you," said Kev.

"Are you sure any of what was there before is still there?"

Sean piped up. "Me and Dad tried at the end of last year. The boat broke down and the current dragged us on the sandbank. We never got close."

Gilo had seen the Humber in full flood. Nights he and Jack had taken the *Marianne* to Read's Island on the spring tide. Reluctant passengers aside, they'd shifted cargo of one sort or another from Grimsby or Goole or Immingham and landed on the island countless times and in all weathers. The sandbanks shifted constantly and the currents with them, but that wasn't the worst of it. There wasn't once he hadn't felt the draw of the place; a dark impulse that made you do things you'd never be capable of anywhere else. He weighed the odds. "You're asking me to do what you can't."

Tasha this time: "Dad told me you'd find a way to get done what needed to get done."

"Whatever you think you'll find there, I guarantee it will be something else. My advice, leave it there."

Patrick found him down by the Haven as the sun went down. An inky dusk settled over the boatyard. "May said you'd be here. She also said, 'tell him, if he fancies showing his face, don't come empty-handed.'"

"I'd have come sooner," said Gilo.

"I know, so does May."

"You been keeping your head down?"

Patrick leaned on the railings next to Gilo. "As instructed. We were told no trading or work to be carried out on the day of Jack Causey's funeral. Close the boatyard. Stay at the site, none of us in town, none welcome at Saint Mary's. There was talk of him lying in state. We'd line up, put our X in the book of remembrance and chuck a quid in his cap for the privilege."

"That bad?"

"You know how it is. Borrowed time, mate. Me and Lorna have had enough. May says she'll come with us."

"Where to?"

"Somewhere we can buy a piece of land they can't kick us off."

After a long silence Gilo said, "The Causeys want me to take them to Read's Island."

"So that's why Des was asking if the *Marianne* was sound."

"And?"

"She'd make it up to Ferriby, if that's what you're worried about, which it shouldn't be. Even the egg-snatchers don't chance landing on Read's this time of year. Not so much low-lying as swamped if the tide's against you."

"Could I get a boat with an outboard in at high tide, from the north side?"

He thought about it. "You don't owe them arseholes anything."

Gilo stood up straight. What he did or didn't owe the Causeys was neither here nor there, the trouble was coming his way. Jack's influence kept the worst from coming to pass. With him gone, it was Gilo's responsibility. This morning in church, then at the cemetery, he'd felt the old man's hands at his back. Now he was hearing his words in the water lapping at the jetty: *A little job I need you to do, boy. Get this settled and we're home easy.*

Gilo felt in his pockets for cash. "Can we stop by the shop? I take it May's still a Gordon's girl?"

By the time Gilo and Patrick arrived at the traveller camp, the only lights came from inside the vans. Some kids had started a bonfire a short distance from the main camp. Across the field, two horses stood silhouetted against the firelight.

He gave a rat-a-tat on May's caravan door. Lorna let them in without saying a word.

"We wondered if you'd be back to see him off," said May. Her eyes shone in the low light. She'd stopped dying her hair and was grey, her plait tied in a royal blue ribbon.

"How you doing Gran?" He hugged her gently. She seemed frail, the strength he used to feel in her embrace no longer there.

She whispered, "I've missed you."

A candle flickered on the table and the radio played quietly. The curtains were new and the seats reupholstered; otherwise, every trinket and vase, every photograph, every cup and plate stood exactly as it had on the day he left.

"Bought you this." Gilo put the bottle on the table.

"We'll have one now, Lorna, love. Easy on the tonic."

They didn't stop at one. By the time Lorna refilled their glasses a third time an hour later, the conversation, which had started with reminiscence of the old days, had moved onto these days and the troubles they brought. May's eyes were shining bright. "Them bastards wanted Gemma's kids locked up for that bloody fire last summer. We all knew who was behind it. No respect, not for us or themselves. Godless shite, the lot of 'em."

Lorna warmed to the theme. "I saw Jeanie Causey in Tesco's."

"She 'ave her teeth in?"

"She did. Wrinkly, though. For her age."

"Because she smokes all them fags." May settled her glass in her lap. Her eyes were closed. She'd want her tea shortly and then bed.

"I'll be off soon," said Gilo.

May got to her feet. "Once round the garden before you go."

She put her arm through Gilo's as they strolled through the camp. "I know you'll think otherwise, but Jack Causey should have seen you right after all you did for him. Letting his boy treat you like that was shameful. If he didn't need you n'more, he ought to have said it to your face. And he bloody did need you."

He felt the weight of her holding onto his arm. "It was time, Gran. Anyway, it's done and I've learned."

"I want things to be settled for you. They've no loyalty. Take what they want and bugger the hindmost."

"I made bad choices. But they were my choices."

"So, you won't be making them again?"

She meant Tasha. "She's playing me, or she isn't. Makes no difference. She won't betray me twice."

"You know her Des is a nark?"

It didn't come as a surprise. "He's the dangerous one."

"Not to you, son."

They walked to where the bonfire's embers glowed warm. The last boy stood guard. May told him to go home.

"Mam says I can't. Me dad's rough."

"Go see Lorna. She'll find you a cup of tea and a bit of toast."

The lad skipped off.

"Lorna and Patrick have looked after me well. They've done what you couldn't. But I would like to see more of you."

"I know. We'll find a way."

She gave his arm a squeeze. "You came to ask for my blessing to go on Read's Island."

"They'll hound us out of the county if I don't. They might anyway."

"That's not the reason, though, is it? Take them if you must, but take care. Jack didn't go there much after you'd gone. I think it scared him and so it should. It's a dark place, son. Make sure to leave the darkness there."

Gilo kissed her on the cheek. She drew him to her and held him. Strength in her embrace this time. In a voice so quiet he thought afterwards that he might have imagined it, she said, 'I'll be with you.'

The following night, an hour after dark, they slipped from the haven out into the Humber. Gilo had watched clouds heavy with rain gather on the north bank throughout the afternoon, knowing they ought to postpone. Kev and Des wouldn't hear of it.

The boat chopped across waves they never saw as Gilo steered into the main channel. He maintained a steady speed upriver. Kev and Des held the boat's grab handles, saying nothing. In sight of the Hope and Anchor lights at South Ferriby Sluice, he eased down the throttle, feeling the incoming tide and wind strengthening at their backs. He skirted the northern channel, mindful of changeable currents easily powerful enough to capsize them.

Read's Island appeared as if out of nowhere. Gilo had planned to bring them round to Jack's favoured mooring – there would be shelter of sorts there, but he missed it on the first pass. Coming back a second time he realised it was below water, a part of the island that belonged to the river. He took a chance, steering into the shallows on the island's north-western edge. When he sensed they were close, he lifted the outboard clear and rowed to shore.

They dragged the boat onto the muddy bank. Gilo stood and checked his bearings, sizing up the land as the wind roared in his ears and a Baltic blast from the North Sea stole his breath. With high tide an hour away and the river flooding the island's eastern shore, by his reckoning they had twenty minutes if they were to get to Jack's hiding place and away without being under water. He led them inland, searching for the firmness underfoot that would tell him they were on the path, conscious a wrong step could find him waist deep and sinking into soft wet mud. He doubted Kev or Des would make much of an effort to pull him free.

The wind intensified, rain siling. Behind him, Des was getting nervous. "Kev, mate, this is insane. Is there not another way?"

Talking now as if Gilo wasn't there.

Kev said, "You got us in this shit. If there was a better way out then we'd have done it. The town wants back what we owe. Them bastards'll finish us otherwise."

"They'll finish you whatever," said Gilo.

They didn't argue.

Just when Gilo thought he'd gone too far, fearing the next step would take him into sinking sand, he tripped over the single course of brick that marked the old herder's cottage. Somewhere close by was the trapdoor to Jack's store. Gilo followed the line of the wall, using his boot to test the ground, listening for the hollow sound of the trapdoor. He crouched and felt for the clasp. It was padlocked. He looked to Kev. "You got the key?"

Kev shone his torch over the trapdoor. "No one told me I needed a key."

"No one told you fuck all, did they? Des, what about you?"

A blank.

The rain drove hard into Gilo's face. They were fifty metres from the South Ferriby lights. The channel was too shallow for boats, too treacherous to cross on foot and now awash, flooding faster than he'd anticipated. A car drove along Sluice Road towards Winteringham, headlights on. It came to a stop.

"Turn off the torch," said Gilo.

They crouched in the darkness, wind moaning around them. Torchlight scanned the island from the shore, the beam falling just short. They waited until the car drove off, heading back the way it came.

"You think they saw?" said Des.

Gilo had no intention of waiting to find out. "I'll go back to the boat, get something to lever off the clasp. The hinges are rusted to shit, even if the padlock holds. Stay here. No lights."

Gilo fetched the screwdriver and hurried back, his eyes never straying from the path. He levered under the trap wall, ripping out the hinge screws, and shone his torch into the open trap. Three black sacks, wrapped tight and taped into a square bulk. This was what they'd come for. He lifted out the first – it was heavier than he'd expected – and shoved it to one side. He looked up at Kev and Des and knew their intention. Thinking they'd take what was in the safe and steal the boat. Leave the river rat on Read's Island to drown, locked in Jack Causey's safe place. Except he'd wrecked the trapdoor hinges and now they weren't sure. One glance at the river swirling around the sandbanks between here and the shore told them they'd never row out, never keep from running aground. The current would take them down.

Gilo called out, his voice coarse and broken. "You two made up your minds?"

Des played as if he didn't understand. "What do you want?"

It was then Gilo noticed the figure of a man moving near the northern shore. Difficult to tell for certain with the rain in his eyes, but he had the bearing and gait of Jack Causey, cap low over his eyes, a shovel on one shoulder, dragging a sack towards where they'd left the boat. Gilo ran after him and called out, "Jack, it's me. Gilo Sweeney." His voice was lost in the wind. He stumbled on blindly, boots squelching in the mud. Through the rain, he caught sight of a second man. Jack turned and started towards him and, for an instant, the clouds parted. A single strip of moonlight revealed Des Birch wading across the flooded ground, sinking deeper with each step, half-stumbling, half-crawling, with Jack closing in behind. Gilo knew what was coming. There was nothing he could do to prevent it. An eerie discordant ringing carried from the east, the note wavering in pitch as if broadcast through the cables on the great bridge, rounding to a siren howl that chilled him to the bone. The moon dipped back behind clouds. Gilo's foot caught in the rutted grass and he pitched headlong, hands reaching out to break the fall. When he looked up, Des and the shadowy figure were nowhere to be seen. Only the boat, a grey shape drifting towards the main run of the river. Gilo staggered to his feet and paddled through the shallows, grabbing at the mooring rope. He wrapped it around his arm and with all his strength heaved the boat as far onto firm ground as he was able.

Kev was on his knees when he got back, hands over his ears, staring at the shore. He dropped his hands. "Des," he said.

"What about him?"

"He shone his torch in the trap like you did. Said he saw bones in there, men's bones. Loads of 'em. He lost it. It was like he was here, but not here. He ran. I tried to stop him. I seen 'im go down, like it swallowed him."

Gilo stared into the trap.

Kev said, "Why was you shouting for me dad?"

"What?"

"I heard you shout him."

Gilo was cold and tired and fuck Kev Causey for making him come out here on a night like this. "Get the bags. We're going."

Gilo steered the boat east, heading for Barton. The wind had eased by the time they rounded the final bend and the Humber Bridge came into view. A light flashed three times on the southern bank at the inlet near the old cement works. Gilo brought the boat in and cut the engine, felt the hard bottom of brick and stone.

Kev said, "What are you doing?"

"Going home."

"We're not through the bridge."

Patrick waited on the shore. "Throw me a rope."

Gilo barely had the strength in him.

Patrick reached out with a boathook and dragged the boat in far enough to secure the rope around an old wooden piling. He helped Kev out with the bags and came back for Gilo. Together they hauled the boat onto the shingle.

"What's going on?" Kev shivered.

Patrick ignored him, speaking to Gilo. "It's like you said. Blue lights everywhere."

"Parkes?"

"He's there. So's she. You want to deal with her now?"

"Another time."

"What about him?"

Kev stood with a sopping package under each arm, the contents spilling in the river.

"He's finished, leave him." Gilo tossed Patrick the one dry package. "We got what we came for."

"In that case, ready when you are. Straight up the road and out."

Gilo shoved the boat back into the river. He and Patrick climbed off the beach onto the path between the brick kilns until they were nothing more than shapes in the darkness.

Author Comment

The River Rat is inspired by the 400-year-old tale of the wolfman of Read's Island. It brings together the dark literature of past and present in a story of greed and revenge on the banks of the Humber.

Aside from the fascination with Read's Island – its origins and ownership down the years; its shapeshifting at the mercy of Humber Estuary tides; and the downright strange events that have taken place there – The River Rat uses its bleakness and remoteness to imagine it as the kind of place where dark deeds go unnoticed.

The story makes reference to the industrial heritage of the Humber and the psychogeography of key locations. I've lived in this part of North Lincolnshire since moving from London over twenty years ago and that feeling of an ongoing conversation with the past is inescapable.

Evidence remains in the weatherworn wooden piles on the riverbank a few hundred yards west of the Humber Bridge. On desolate winter mornings when the fog is at its thickest, the wooden spars and pilings of a wrecked jetty stick out from the sucking mud. On those mornings it feels like a haunted place.

There is also the link with Ted Lewis's 1970 novel *Jack's Return Home*, adapted and directed by Mike Hodges as the genre-defining revenge thriller *Get Carter* in 1971. The novel is set mainly in the steel town of Scunthorpe, but its climactic scenes take place at derelict brick kilns near the Humber where

Lewis and his childhood friends once played out stories inspired by 1950s gangster films and B-movies.

Then as now, Read's Island, the Humber foreshore, and its abandoned industrial works are vivid and evocative settings for the imagination. Ideal for an outsider story of revenge, betrayal, power, and smalltown corruption.

THE HOLBEACH CARDIES

John Gallas

"Dear owd Codling's gone an' up an' deed."
"O how shall we play oor whists without 'im now?"
"For Three don't make a Four, an' niver will."
Oi poked the fire, an' made the clock stand still.

"Oi know! Less go an' play 'im one last time."
"A kind o' whistful 'membrance in 'is name!"
"A kind o' Dead Man's Hand ter say godbye!"
Oi lit 'em to the Church acraws the High.

"Lift 'im out boys. Prop 'im on the pew."
"Don't look right dead, do ee, sittin' there?"
"Just like ole times, eh, boys? Deal away!"
Oi sped the clock. Oi made a holyday.

"Owd Codling's playin' better than afoor!"
"'Tis good ter see 'im all agirn agin!"
"'Is 'and's on fire! Ee's got the Divil's Luck!"
Oi gagged the Saints an' Angels. Midnight struck.

"Bless me, 'ow time flies! Just one last 'and."
"Mappen there be 'orns on Codling's 'ed."
"Mappen that there's werms come out 'is nose."
An' then oi burst 'im reetly. So it goes.

"Oh! Oh! My brain! What be this tide o' blood?"
"Oh! Oh! My skull is splet! An' splet agin!"
"Oh! Oh! What be this blade that cricks an' cracks?"
A Heart. A Club. A Spade. A bloody Axe.

SOMEWHERE DOWN DAWSPOND GATE

John Gallas

Somewhere down Dawspond Gate
a small sealed track just wide enough for one
runs straight between two sheepfields
through to Fenland Air, like the join of an opened book.

I've never found it again, but the day that it was there
I pedalled along in slow, slow wise under a page of
    brownbright cloud
while organpipes of wind played sideways at me
where the hedgerows' thorny gaps made Os of ochre light.

I stopped because I lost my way. I mean, my *usual* way: as if
I biked along a ruler no one ever cut a measure on, *moving nowhere.*
Then I saw *them.* Five heads bobbing up the road at me
like soft piston-pins driving the engine of their – *was it?* – song.

They came… and went: in billycock hats, applecheeked, in
    cordy-breeches,
smocks and boots: a scythe, a crook, a rake: one fiddle and a
    choir of four.
I said hello. They touched their hats, but heedlessly in their
    harmonies,

and left agog I watched their backs grow tiny and their tenors
    blow away.

Byway or highway, let me say it is not *my* way
to tear at the Vasty Veil of Time, or conjure spooks
from out of my biking brain: oh they were there alright,
five hardy complications in plain sight.

At Fenland Air the little biplanes
blustered in the browny rack, and bounced back
down to earth along the neat green folios of
their landingstrips into the wind. I pedalled on,

wondering from time to time which world I laboured in.
Eight miles home, the waypost said.
Contrary now, the gusty weather
resisted my return to Holbeach Hurn.

THE BALLAD OF THE MAN IN THE PLASTIC CHAIR IN THE SOUTH HOLLAND MAIN DRAIN WHERE IT CROSSES HORSEMOOR DROVE NEAR SUTTON ST JAMES

John Gallas

Under the pylons and past the new farm
with a concrete pig on the lawn,
just where the bridge goes over the drove
I heard the whoop of a horn.

I got off my bike and looked over the bank.
Nothing stirred in the Drain.
A gnome with a fishing-rod further down
sat still as a stump in the rain.

Stuck on the rail, there's a small metal plaque
in memory of 'Goozler' MacBet,
'Who Cared For the South Holland Drains all his life:
and may he watch over them Yet.'

And *tan-tan-taraa*! I heard it again.
But tinny and faint, like a toy.

Way down the water, and way past the gnome,
something was moving. *Ahoy*!

Ahoy! I shouted. I put down my bike.
The mist cleared a little – and there,
just pointed out with a finger of sun –
was a man in a plastic chair!

He was paddling about with a paper plate,
and blowing the *Lonesome Hen*,
with a pair of binoculars round his neck,
and a map, and a pad, and a pen.

He paddled away to the vanishing point,
where the air was brighter – and *whish!*
he kind of *dispersed* in the drizzly sky.
The gnome continued to fish:

and I got back on my bike – and wondered
if that was 'Goozler' MacBet,
who cared all his life for the heavenly drains
and was watching over them Yet.

In Sutton St James, The Feathers was shut.
The clock on the church said ten.
I headed for home with my blinkers on
and the moon over Moorswood Fen.

Author Comment

These three poems/tales are all pedal-related. I visit my caravan near Sutton St James every darned week for a couple of day's biking, moseying & wandering (*'Not all those who wander are lost'*). The Dawspond Sighting was spooky and real; the Watcher of the Drains has his little memorial welded to a nearby bridge; the Holbeach cardplayers *dealt with the Devil* in the church just next to a very handy, oft-visited, rare-in-these-parts, cash machine.

When you are zipping through a freezing morning Gedney Hill fog, and the new sun turns the drains into bars of gold, and the tiny rattle of the bike chain sets off Mexican waves of ducks, swans, pheasants, crows, hares, larks, muntjacs and dog-barks, it isn't hard to believe you've torn through the 'Vasty Veil of Time'.

GLOSSARY

Though by no means exhaustive, this anthology showcases something of the breadth of Lincolnshire folk tales. Most of the contributions build upon established folk tales, legends, or partial evidence for 'lost' folk tales in extant sources, in which case we have provided brief notes on tales and sources, presented in the order in which they appear in the book. Two of John Gallas's three contributions to this anthology have no direct connection to extant folk tales, but conjure new ones out of the landscape.

ANWICK DRAKE STONE

The Anwick Drake Stone comprises two rounded hunks of Spilsby sandstone on the grass outside the churchyard to St Edith's church in Anwick. This was a bigger singular stone until early in the last century, and is still often referred to in the singular.

Initially located in a nearby field, the Drake Stone legendarily marked the location of a treasure hoard, guarded either by the Devil, demons, or a winged dragon. Reverend George Oliver, writing in the early nineteenth century, noted that 'There was a running tradition' that the stone had been placed in its original location 'to indicate the presence of treasure which had been buried on the spot', where it was 'under the especial protection of the Devil'.[1] According to tradition, attempts to move it were futile.

None of this is unique to Anwick. Large stones, including glacial erratics and prehistoric monuments, are often alleged to be immovable, or otherwise to curse those who do manage to move them. Big stones were also often alleged to mark buried treasure, regularly protected by a sort of guard-demon. They were then often moved from fields in the early twentieth century, when machinery had grown and superstitions had waned.

There are various theories about its name. Adrian Gray suggests 'drake' may be a corruption of 'dragon', which points to the name having Brythonic origins ('draig' is Welsh for 'dragon').[2] David Clark gives a more probable and mundane explanation: as the rock was a hazard to ploughing, a farmer dug a trench around it in an attempt to sink it 'to a safe level', creating a pond that filled with water and attracted ducks.[3] Writing in the 1930s, not long after the stone had been moved, Ethel Rudkin posited that the name is 'likely' to be used 'in the same sense as the expression "Fire Drakes," for the flickery Northern Lights', though she does not substantiate this.[4] It is also sometimes said that it used to look like a drake's head.

GIBBERY GAP

Gibbery Gap is an old colloquial name for a break in a hedge that runs along what is now Caistor Road, at a crossroads, near the North Lincolnshire village of Kirmington. According to an almost entirely forgotten legend, a Royalist soldier, slashed in the stomach, attempted to escape through the Gap, holding his entrails in with his cap, and died before reaching Kirmington. There is no recorded battlefield in the close vicinity. Nonetheless, this was commemorated in a couplet that may be part of a longer, lost poem or folk song, which is quoted in Brackenbury's sequence: 'From Micklow Hill to Gibbery Gap / He carried his puddings in his cap.' There are two supernatural anecdotes regarding Gibbery Gap: that the soldier's spectral form can still occasionally be seen crossing the road and going through the break in the hedge; and that nothing can grow where the soldier passed, hence the gap in the hedge persisting.[5]

The earliest known textual reference to Gibbery Gap is in the diaries of the folklorist Ethel Rudkin, who gives the location that name (but mentions neither the soldier's story nor the rhyme) in entries in 1930 and 1956.[6] Ordnance Survey maps do not and never have used it, though it clearly was once in use locally. The name may come from the verb 'gib', meaning 'to gut', specifically referring to fish.

HAXEY HOOD

The Haxey Hood is a game played on the Twelfth Day of Christmas, in and between the villages of Haxey and Westwoodside on the Isle of Axeholme. Ethel Rudkin (1936) wrote an account of the game as it unfolded in 1932.[7] Almost a century later, it is still essentially the same.

The game may originate as far back as the fourteenth century, and has the following legend attached to it to explain that origin. Lady de Mowbray, wife of the local landowner, lost her hood while riding home. Thirteen labourers rushed to retrieve it, and did so. However, the first was too shy to give the garment back, so she called him a 'fool'. The second was less timid, earning the soubriquet 'lord'. As a reward, Lady de Mowbray gave thirteen acres of land to the local community on the condition that the event would be reenacted every year.

It is likely that the legend grew to explain event. If so, its real origins have been lost to history. The objective of the game is to push the hood, in fact a dense leather tube, from the field behind the church in Haxey to the door of one of four nearby pubs (three in Haxey and one in Westwoodside), where it stays proudly on display until the following year. The 'fool' and 'lord' monickers are preserved in the names of two of the game's officials, which also include eleven 'boggins' (including a chief boggin). The game itself is open to anyone who wants to join in, which results in robust crowds swaying through the lanes and streets, usually well into the night, singing folk songs as steam rises from them, the hood hidden somewhere in the middle, and clusters of onlookers following at a moderately safe distance.

THE BELVOIR WITCHES

The trial of the Belvoir (or sometimes Bottesford) Witches is one of the best-known witchcraft trials in the country. It involved the Manners family, whose seat was Belvoir Castle on the Lincolnshire-Leicestershire border, and three women – Joan Flower and her two daughters Margaret and Phillip (recorded by later authors as Philippa or Phillis) – who were employed as maids at Belvoir. Thought of as loose, ill-tempered, and untrustworthy by co-workers, the women were accused of causing the illness and death of the Manners' two male heirs, Henry and Frances, and of preventing their parents from conceiving more children. The words at the end of Jane

Simmons' poem are lifted directly from one of the Manners' tombs in Bottesford, Nottinghamshire.

The accusations were enough to see the women to trial at the Lincoln assizes. On their way to Lincoln, forty miles away, they stopped for the night at the village of Ancaster. There, Joan asked for bread and butter, allegedly declared that it would not pass through her if she were guilty of witchcraft, then promptly choked and died. At Lincoln, the two daughters confessed to performing malefic witchcraft on behalf of themselves and their mother, and they were executed on 11 March 1618.

The trial was recorded in an anonymous contemporary pamphlet, *The Wonderful Discoverie of the Witchcrafts of Margaret and Phillip Flower, Daughters of Joan Flower Neere Beuer Castle* (1619), and commemorated in a ballad, *Damnable Practises of Three Lincolnshire Witches Joane Flower and Her Two Daughters*, published the same year. While both pamphlet and ballad state that Joan Flowers requested bread and butter, some time before the eighteenth century her desire for food transmuted into a request for the eucharist, lending a more explicitly supernatural dimension to her alleged demise. If bread blessed by a priest stuck in the woman's throat, then surely her crime was an affront to God himself. Marion Gibson (2000) provides an historical account of the trial.[8]

THE LINCOLN IMP

Possibly the best-known grotesque in England, the Lincoln Imp is a tiny thirteenth-century cross-legged carving in the Angel Choir and above the tomb of St Hugh in Lincoln Cathedral, overlooking the altar. While grotesques are obviously common, nobody is quite sure why a little devilish-looking creature has been situated in the most sacred part of the building.

There are many variations of a folk tale that seek to explain it, the earliest of which is a poem by Arnold Frost, published in 1897, which he claims to have collected from a man in his sixties in North Lincolnshire, who heard it as a boy.[9] Most renditions agree that he was sent on a supernatural wind conjured by Satan to wreak mischief, but was caught either by an angel or the bishop and turned to stone. The wind still waits for its rider in the cathedral yard, justifying the location's often blustery conditions. Another 'imp' is on the cathedral exterior, and some variants incorporate this into the original. Further variants suggest an imp-like carving in Grimsby Minster is his coeval, who initially escaped and was then turned to stone there. Yet more variants suggest the imp (or imps) caused mayhem elsewhere on their way to Lincoln, e.g. by twisting the crooked spire at Chesterfield in Derbyshire.

The grotesque's design was popularised by the jewellers James Usher & Son, who took out a patent in 1890. Since then, versions of the imp have regularly been adopted as symbols or mascots by a range of local establishments, including Lincoln City Football Club (nicknamed the Imps) and Lincolnshire County Council.

THE TETFORD WITCH

Women all over England were, until fairly recently, accused of witchcraft or at least suspected of being witches. Gutch and Peacock (1908) provide many examples in Lincolnshire. One lived in a cottage near Tetford's parish church that had a 'cat hole', through which it was said she could enter and leave in the form of a cat or a hare. She supposedly killed her children and sister, and led a neighbour into decrepitude so that he was unable to work. One day, when this neighbour was out walking with a friend, the two of them saw a hare standing on its hind legs. The friend shot at the animal, wounding it, but it escaped. In a trope common in witch tales, the hare-form's injuries were transferred to the witch when she shifted back, and Mrs E. took to her bed covered in spreading boils or 'breaders'. In another version of the tale, the hare was shot in the leg, and Mrs E. was only able to recover by rubbing the wound with the sawn-off hind leg of a hedgehog.

Variants of this story are recorded by James Alpass Penny (1922) and Mary Borrows (1986).[10] Susanna O'Neill (2012) notes the frequency with which witches shapeshift into animals, especially hares, in the folklore of Lincolnshire, but it is a common trope nationally.[11] Nonetheless, Paweł Rutkowski (2019) argues that witches-turned-animals were more common on the continent than in England, where a witch was more likely to resort to the aid of a familiar spirit in animal disguise than to assume that disguise herself.[12]

ST. OSWALD AND THE SHAFT OF LIGHT

In Lincolnshire, a person who does not close a door might be asked 'Do you come from Bardney?', or something similar. The origin of this is the apparent result of a miracle at Bardney (Beardeneau) Abbey, a Benedectine monastery founded by King Æthelred of Mercia in 697. Bede recounts that the Mercian queen Osthryth was fond of the abbey and bestowed most of the relics of her uncle, St Oswald, upon it. The monks initially declined to take them in: Oswald, King of Northumbria, had conquered Lindsey and was essentially regarded as a foreigner. The relics remained overnight on a wagon outside the gate, but a pillar of light shone from it to the heavens. The monks responded by accepting the relics and built a dedicated shrine for them; the water that was used to wash them developed healing properties. The abbot at the time also reportedly commanded all locks to be removed from the doors.[13] The prevalence of the saying has effectively allowed this fairly standard religious miracle to enter secular folk tradition as a means of explaining it, though nobody knows for how long the saying has been used.

In addition to being the focus of Jane Simmons' poem, miracles associated with Oswald are alluded to in the second part of Alex Harvey's 'The Hood'. The editors of this anthology have been unable to identify 'Rory summat-or-other', have nothing else to say on the matter, and ask readers not to give it any thought whatsoever.

MAIDENWELL

Maidenwell is a depopulated village in East Lindsey, just south of Louth. One (spurious) explanation for its etymology, recorded in a reader's letter in the magazine *Lincolnshire Life* (1975), is that a young woman was thrown down a well by Cromwell's soldiers. Ethel Rudkin (1936) includes this brief entry: 'In Ostler's Lane there is a haunting – a coach and horses goes by, and the coachman has his head on the box beside him.'[14]

EAST HALTON HOBTHRUST

Hobthrusts, hobthrushes, hobhursts or, simply, hobs, are diminutive household spirits, legends about which are prevalent in the English North and Midlands. They often reputedly assist with domestic and farmyard chores, but can be quick to take offence, and once offended can turn malicious. A helpful household sprite is often referred to as a brownie, and Jacqueline Simpson and Steve Roud (2000) refer to this story in their dictionary entry for that term.[15]

This particular hobthrust attaches himself to a farm in East Halton. He is first noticed when the farmer goes to round up the sheep for shearing, only to find that they are already gathered in the barn, together with a hare; the hobthrust complains that the 'grey sheep' had been much more difficult to round up than the others. Hobthrust and farmer then broker a deal that the hob will help with farmyard tasks, and in return the farmer will give him a shirt of good linen every New Year's Eve. This arrangement continues amicably for some time, until one year the farmer decides to leave a shirt of sack-cloth instead. Offended by being shortchanged, the hobthrust abandons the farm and soon it falls into disrepair.

One of the earliest allusions in print to this tale comes from Mabel Peacock in 1901, who augments the story with beliefs about human interaction with the hobthrust:

He has attached himself to a house in the parish of
East-Halton. The stories which are generally
related of his northern relative are told of him too,
but he is distinguished by one idiosyncrasy. He may
always be made to 'walk' by stirring the contents of
an iron pot in the cellar, which pot is supposed to
contain 'children's thumb-bones.'[16]

The folklorist Maureen James tells a version of the tale, and
notes that the East Halton hobthrust is connected to other
more local stories; one tells of how the villagers tried to build
a church, but at night the hobthrust would destroy their work,
so in the end it had to be built south of the village.[17] This is a
variation on a common legend: throughout England, the
remote locations of some churches, in relation to the villages
they were built to serve, was said to be the result of malevolent
forces repeatedly destroying the building or moving the stones
until the builders relented.

THE FONABY SACK STONE

This used to be a stack of three stones that resembled a sack
of grain, near Fonaby Top, a couple of miles from the ancient
town of Caistor. According to legend, either Christ or the
missionary St Paulinus (who did indeed help to bring
Christianity to Lindsey) was undertaking an arduous journey
on his ass when he spotted a farmer sowing corn, opencast
from a sack. Christ or Paulinus asked whether the farmer
would spare some corn for his animal, but the farmer replied
that the sack contained only stones. Intent on teaching the
farmer a lesson, Christ/Paulinus promptly transformed the

sack into stone and continued on his journey.

It was said to be unlucky to mess with the Sack Stone in any way. For example, according to legend, a mason working on the construction of the nearby Pelham Pillar in the 1840s chipped a flake from the Sack Stone with the intention of incorporating it into the structure, and subsequently broke his neck.

Not unlike the Anwick Drake Stone, discussed above, the Fonaby Sack Stone supposedly took twenty-two horses to move from its original spot, but, after a period of misfortune, only one lame nag was required to move it back. In the 1910s it was, however, moved more permanently to the edge of the field, where some of its constituent parts can still just about be seen poking through the soil and undergrowth. Ethel Rudkin (1936) discusses the legend, and provides a photograph from 'about 1890', when the stones were still stacked in the field, alongside two she had taken herself in 1933 that show the rocks side by side below a hedge, in a much better state of preservation than they are today. According to Rudkin, in that year 'it was arranged to restore the Sack Stone and set it up again, but when it came to the point and the men went to do it, the farmer refused to let them touch it'.[18]

THE HALTON HOLEGATE HAUNTING

This ghost story was made popular in the late 1890s. For example, in 1897, the notoriously sensationalist *Illustrated Police News* (mentioned in Robert Etty's poem) ran a story about a ghost terrorising a farm in Halton Holegate, disturbing the inhabitants Mr and Mrs Wilson and their unnamed servant, with the noises of furniture moving and the apparition of a stooped old man. Mrs Wilson then made a 'gruesome discovery' in the sitting room:

> The floor in one corner had been very uneven, and
> a day or two ago Mrs. Wilson took up the bricks
> with the intention of relaying them. No sooner had
> she done this than a most disagreeable odour war
> emitted. Her suspicions being aroused, she called
> her husband, and the two commenced a minute
> examination. Three or four bones were soon turned
> over, together with a gold ring and several pieces of
> old black silk. All these had evidently been buried in
> quick-lime.[19]

Following this discovery, the spectre of the old man was not seen again, but the uncanny noises continued to occur. The story was followed up by James John Hissey, who visited the farmhouse in 1898 and interviewed Mr and Mrs Wilson. He left disappointed: 'no high-spirited or proper-minded ghost, we felt, would have anything to do with such a place, and presuming that he existed, he at once fell in our estimation – we despised him!' After an unconvincing tour, and with 'a sense of disappointment amounting almost to disillusion, we departed.'[20]

MARKBY CHURCH

Markby St Peter's is, as Philippa East's story says, the only thatched church in Lincolnshire. It was built in 1611 on the site of the dissolved Markby Priory, using some of the stone from the ruin and incorporating several of its carvings.

There is a superstition that if a person runs three times anticlockwise around the church and bangs a nail into the church door, they'll see a ghost. There are, correspondingly, many holes and stubs of nails in the door, most of them obviously very old.

Circling a church anticlockwise, or widdershins (as opposed to deosil, sunwise/clockwise), is considered unlucky across much of Europe, and circling a religious building clockwise is a common rite in many religions, e.g. Buddhism, Sikhism, Hinduism and Jainism. In Britain, the notion that circling a church widdershins was unlucky remained 'purely a Scottish and Irish belief' until the nineteenth century, according to Jacqueline Simpson and Steve Roud, but subsequently it became more widespread in folk belief.[21] A person moving in this manner may expect anything from meeting ghosts or the Devil to being transported to Fairyland.

TIDDY MUN

This 'tiddy', i.e. small, man 'without a name' and sounding like a peewit, was a supernatural keeper of the fenland landscape of the Carrs in the valley of the River Ancholme, which flows northwards into the Humber. According to a tale told to Marie Clothilde Balfour in the 1880s, locals used to appeal to him in times of flood, which he was always able to avert. With the draining of the Carrs, however, Tiddy Mun was forgotten, which was believed to have resulted in destructive floods and illnesses. Once the locals returned to propitiating him, things got back to normal and soon all was 'thrivin' i' tha' Cars'.[22] Today, Tiddy Mun reads as a potent folk image of environmental change and degradation, a notion explored by Darwin Horn (1987) with reference to the ecological effects of drainage and how they affect people, animals and buildings.[23]

The legend has also to some extent been adopted, belatedly, across the Fens in and beyond southern Lincolnshire. It is not unlikely that counterpart legends once existed across England's eastern flatlands, but Tiddy Mun's origins are specifically in the north-west of the county. A modern road bridge near Guyhirn in Cambridgeshire, a few miles south of the Lincolnshire border and a long way from the River Ancholme, has been given the name Tiddy Mun Bridge.

TOM OTTER

This twenty-eight-year-old Nottinghamshire-born navvy, working in Lincoln and apparently using his mother's maiden name of Temporal or Temporel, was convicted in 1806 of murdering Mary Kirkham and their unborn child, hanged in Lincoln that March, and subsequently gibbeted on what is now Tom Otter Lane, near Saxilby. A sensationalist account by Thomas Miller, published in the *Lincoln Times* in 1959, cemented the case's legendary status: among other reports of supernatural events, after Kirkham's body was removed to a the Sun Inn in Saxilby (which still exists), it was said that the sounds of a child crying could always be heard in the room where the body had been kept, and the Foss Dyke had supposedly run red when Otter's corpse had been taken across it. But despite Miller's painting of Tom Otter as a heinous murderer, and his notoriety as the last criminal to be gibbetted in Lincolnshire, the initial evidence used to accuse him was circumstantial.

Having made Kirkham pregnant in 1805, Otter was forced to marry her in a 'knob-stick wedding' in South Hykeham that November, by authorities who were unaware that he already had a wife and child back home in Nottinghamshire. Later that day, and for reasons unknown, Otter and the heavily-pregnant Kirkham walked to and beyond Saxilby, about ten miles from South Hykeham. Then, on the roadside near Drinsey Nook, Mary was beaten to death with a hedge-stake. Miller claimed to have discovered the death-bed testimony of a local labourer called John Dunberley or Dunkerly, purporting to have seen the murder take place. Dunberley also allegedly claimed that, every year on the anniversary of the murder, Otter and Kirkham would reappear to him in spectral form. They would then force him to steal the hedge-stake, take it to the scene of the crime, and commit the murder in Otter's stead.

Otter's body was denied a Christian burial, in accordance with the 1751 Murder Act, and remained in the gibbet near Drinsey Nook until the structure was blown down in a storm in 1850. Gypsies, described prejudicially by two of the Victorian characters in Zouroudi's narrative, were said to have set up camp near to it.[24] In 1811, birds had nested in Otter's skull, inspiring this folk rhyme:

> There were ten tongues within one head;
> And one went out to fetch some bread
> To feed the living in the dead.[25]

This is a variant of what was once a common feature of a riddle-tale, of a type known as 'Out-riddling the Judge', in which a defendant is able to be set free if he can pose a riddle that a judge is unable to solve. The riddle typically concerns several tongues in one head, the answer to which is a nest of chicks in a horse's skull. The irony of applying this instead to the head of an executed convict is obvious.

The case has prompted, and continues to prompt, numerous retellings, in both story and song. Most nonfiction accounts of what happened assume Dunberley's testimony is genuine, even if they question the veracity of its supernatural elements.[26]

YALLERY BROWN

'Yallery Brown' is one of the ten tales collected by Marie Clothilde Balfour and first published in the journal *Folklore* in 1891, in a gallantly-attempted approximation of the local dialect. Balfour was Scottish, and lived in Redbourne, a village in the Ancholme Valley, near Kirton in Lindsey. 'Yallery Brown' is unusual among the tales Balfour collected, because it is told by a named protagonist in the first person, and because it is specifically set in and around the village of Redbourne, referring to several clearly identifiable local landmarks. Joseph Jacobs brought the tale to a wider readership in *More English Fairy Stories* (1894), though he removed almost all the dialect, changed some parts of the setting, and gave the story a third-person narrator.

Maureen James, in her 2013 PhD thesis *Investigating the Legends of the Carrs*, suggests the protagonist of Balfour's rendition of the tale, who gives his name only as Tom, might have been a farm labourer called Thomas Laming, who worked at a farm nearby.

Some other folklorists suspect Balfour might have made up part or even all of the tale, because the story has no direct analogues (beyond its obvious connection to the 'spirit in the bottle' tale type), which is unusual for a folk tale. It is notable that she was a budding novelist who went on to publish several novels.

There are many more recent versions of 'Yallery Brown' in print, all in prose, all published since the late 1960s when Alan Garner included a rendition in *A Book of Goblins* (1969). It is now, therefore, one of the better-known folk tales associated with Lincolnshire. Mick Gowar invents or 'alters' some details in his 2004 version written for schoolchildren, including the tale's ending, and sets it in Suffolk. Almost all other versions keep very close to the original in plot and setting.

THE DEAD HAND

Collected by Marie Clothilde Balfour in or near Redbourne, near Kirton in Lindsey, 'The Dead Hand' is included in the second instalment of her 'Legends of the Lincolnshire Cars' (1891), in which all tales are written in the Scottish woman's hearty but inconsistent approximation of the local dialect. It includes two elements prevalent elsewhere in the tales Balfour collected in this area: the supernaturally dangerous landscape of the marshy Carrs (as it is now written), populated by boggarts, sprites and the spirits of the dead, and the focus on an intrepid but foolish young man who gets himself into trouble with the marsh's otherworldly denizens.

Tom Pattison, unlike his friends, decides to disregard protective charms procured by his mother when crossing the

Carrs on the darkest night of the year. His friends watch in horror as the wind snuffs out his lantern and all manner of supernatural creatures descend upon him. Finally, a disembodied hand pulls him under the water. The other lads, protected by their mothers' keepsakes, make it home unscathed. A week later, Tom is found at the spot where he vanished, white-haired and shaking, his feet submerged, with one hand missing, and (terminally, as it turns out) unable to speak: 'ther wor nobbut a ragged bleedin' stump – th' han' 'd bin pulled clean off! An' theer a sat, gibbering, girnin', an' grinnin' at th' horrors, as nobbut hisself cud see!'[27] A year later, mother and son are found dead – she with a look of serenity and he with one of horror. Thereafter, they haunt the area.

'The Dead Hand' is often included in folk tale collections. For example, versions appear in Kevin Crossley-Holland's *Long Tom and the Dead Hand: More Tales from East Anglia and the Fen Country* (1992) and in *The Old Stories: Folk Tales from East Anglia and the Fen Country* (1999), and Polly Howat's *Ghosts & Legends of Lincolnshire and the Fen Country* (1992) and *Tales from the Misty Fen* (1994). As with some other tales originally collected by Balfour, Crossley-Holland's inclusion of a version of this story in a collection of East Anglian tales has helped to encourage a recent belief that it is a folk tale from that area.

THE POTTLE O' BRAINS

This tale was also collected by Marie Clothilde Balfour in or near Redbourne, and included in the second instalment of her 'Legends of the Lincolnshire Cars' (1891). It concerns a young man who goes out in search of a pottle (pitcher) of brains because he is tired of being a fool. He solicits the advice of a local wisewoman, and she instructs him to bring her the heart of whatever or whomever he loves most. He tries three times, bringing her, consecutively, the heart of a pig (on account of his love of bacon), his recently deceased mother's corpse, and – after he subsequently meets and marries her – his new bride. On his first two return visits, the wisewoman poses the young man a riddle, but he is unable to answer, showing that he hasn't yet found his brains. The third time, his wife whispers the solution in his ear, and the wisewoman declares that the young man has found his pottle of brains: they are in his wife's head.

The story's collector, Marie Clothilde Balfour (1891), identifies it as a 'droll', a tale about local people or events that conveyed some moral lesson as well as providing entertainment.[28] The tale is included in Joseph Jacobs' *More English Fairy Tales* (1892) and Katharine Briggs' *British Folk Tales* (1970). It remains fairly popular, and offers good storytellers the opportunity at once to pull heartstrings and hit funny-bones.

THE LASS WHO SAW HER OWN GRAVE DUG

In this tale, a lad called Fox courts a girl called Bessie, with sudden and apparently huge devotion, and arranges to meet her by a remote tree. The night before they are to meet, Bessie has a strange premonitory dream, so she decides to get to the tree early, climb it and hide, and see what he is up to. Fox arrives a little after, digs a grave, waits, then fills it back in and leaves when he concludes that she isn't coming. The following day, he turns up at her door and asks why she flaked on him, and she responds with a riddle that isn't exactly cryptic, which includes these lines: 'Th' leaves did shake, / My heart did aache / to sea th' hoale / Th' fox did maake'. He tries to run but is apprehended by Bess's father and several other men, and taken to prison.

Variants of this tale are local to many parts of England; Katharine M. Briggs (1970) tells several variants, and notes that 'This is one of the commonest of English legends'.[29] It was collected by Mabel Peacock (1886), from whom the above quotation in dialect is taken.[30] Maureen James (2013) puts it into modern standard English, and notes that the narrator 'said that the story was set in Buslingthorpe' – once a substantial village, but largely depopulated since the seventeenth century, and now comprising a small cluster of farms and cottages beside the earthworks of part of the medieval settlement.[31]

It is a version of what is sometimes referred to as 'the Robber Bridegroom tale', perhaps best known in a variant from the Brothers Grimm's *Kinder und Hausmärchen* (1812), in which the main characters are a prince and princess, and the subsequent 1857 edition, in which the protagonists are commoners. 'Mr Fox', in turn, is included by Joseph Jacobs in his compilation *English Fairy Tales* (1890). Here, a young lady has a promontory dream that she goes to her suitor's castle and makes a series of terrible discoveries, which prove to be true, so 'her brothers and her friends drew their swords and cut Mr. Fox into a thousand pieces.'[32]

While the Robber Bridegroom tale generally does not go into much detail about the bridegroom's previous victims, the

Lincolnshire variant in particular sits alongside several tales of women murdered or abandoned by their sweethearts and forced to haunt the place of their demise. Juliet E. McKenna mentions three of them: the Black Lady of Bradley Woods, the Irby Boggle, and Tom Otter's murder of Mary Kirkham – the latter (which is discussed earlier in these gloss notes) being an historical event mythologised into a gory shocker. With these stories largely overlooking the female victims of intimate partner violence, or consigning them to the role of passive ghosts doomed to wait for other people to seek justice on their behalf, 'The Lass that Saw Her Own Grave Dug' is a refreshing example of female agency.

BOGGARTS

Boggarts are elusive supernatural creatures. Simon Young (2022) defines 'boggart' as 'a generic term to describe the solitary supernatural creatures that terrified the English North and parts of the Midlands in Victorian (and in some cases later) times.'[33] Curiously, he places the term quite late, even though the word and its cognates boggard and boggle are recorded in use since at least the 1570s. Young also supplies several contemporary accounts from Lincolnshire, among which the following stands out particularly:

> I don't think my Grandma considered boggarts as fairies; I never heard her use that word in Connection with them, she spoke of them more as we would ghosts or ghouls, and considered them a nuisance.[34]

It seems boggarts belong to that nebulous 'other crowd' that exists alongside humankind, but cannot easily be categorised.

Marie Clothilde Balfour (1891) seems equally reticent to pigeonhole boggarts: she writes of them – and quotes people talking of them – as malicious entities stalking unwary travellers in the waterlogged Carrs around the River Ancholme, but also, potentially, as the 'strangers' or 'tiddy people' who look after the landscape and are propitiated by the locals. The present anthology contains a range of boggart-type characters, including Tiddy Mun and Yallery Brown, reflecting something of their multifaceted nature.

HAVELOK AND GRIM

These characters are best known from the late twelfth-century middle English romance *Havelok the Dane*, though earlier Anglo-Norman accounts exist. The romance tells of two dispossessed royal heirs – of Denmark and of England – who go through a variety of adventures before being restored to their birthrights. The life of the Danish prince Havelok also serves as the foundation myth of Grimsby, the principal town on the northern Lincolnshire coast. The tale has held meaning for the town since at least the thirteenth century, when Havelok, Grim and another character, Goldeboru, were depicted on the town seal.

READ'S ISLAND WEREWOLF

Read's Island lies off the coast of North Lincolnshire in the Humber Estuary. Uninhabited and essentially uninhabitable, it is currently a nature reserve managed by the RSPB. However, the island does show signs of past human activity. The earliest mention of Read's Island seems to be on the Customs Map of 1734, where it is shown as a sandbank called Old Warp (potentially after the practice of 'warping', manoeuvring a turbid river to deposit a layer of silt in a desirable location). Towards the end of the eighteenth century, grass was growing on the island in large enough quantities to support cattle. It has since been occupied by humans, such as in the 1860s when a sheep farmer called William Foster lived there with his family. The island also served as a bird-shooting reserve. The last occupier moved away in 1989, and all permanent structures, threatened by erosion, have since been demolished.

The island was once the alleged home of the so-called Read's Island wolfman. The tale goes that some four centuries ago, a man set up a rough shelter on the island and earned his keep by ferrying people across the Humber. Soon, scores of locals began to go missing. Suspicion fell on the ferryman, who was taken to court, accused of murdering and cannibalising his victims. The accusations were said to have been proven correct when it was discovered that Read's Island was littered with human remains. 'During his trial in East Yorkshire,' notes Daniel Codd (2007), he allegedly 'collapsed vomiting on to all fours, howling like an animal [and began] to take on the form of a monstrous wolf.'[35]

The Read's Island wolfman finds himself in the company of other folkloric werewolves or werewolf-like beings in Lincolnshire: Old Mother Nightshade, a witch who lived near Gedney Dyke and allegedly took the shape of a wolf to devour her victims; and the Langrick Werewolf, a body of a man with a wolf's head allegedly unearthed on Langrick Fen, his discovery temporarily rousing the werewolf's ghost to walk again.

THE HOLBEACH GAMESTERS

This is the tale of three men who were playing cards in the Chequers Inn, Holbeach (which closed a few years ago), and talking about a friend who had recently died, so they decided to dig him up and play cards with him in the church opposite. This seems really to have happened, in 1783 or 1793, though it soon entered the realms of folklore. One legend has it that passers-by after dark might see lights flickering in the windows, and that they signal the ghosts of the gamesters, who had been dragged to hell by demons that fateful night.

John Gallas's 'The Holbeach Cardies' has earlier poetic counterparts. In 1800, i.e. not all that long after the event had apparently taken place, Thomas Hardwicke Rawnsley published a ballad called 'The Three Revellers, or Impiety Punished: A Legend of Holbeach', which ends rather fantastically:

> "What silent, my Dumby, when most I you need
>   Dame Fortune our wishes has crossed,"
> When a voice from beneath, howled, "your fate is decreed
>   The game and the gamesters are lost."
>
> Then strange! most terrific and horrid to view!
>   Three Demons thro' earth burst their way:
> Each one chose his partner, his arms round him threw
>   And vanished in smoke with his prey.[36]

A perhaps even more intriguing counterpart is 'The Sacrilegious Gamesters' (1843), also a ballad, by the once-popular Victorian poet and Chartist Eliza Cook. In this poem, the dead gamester is described as having 'died in the midst of his career, / As the sinful ever die; / without one prayer from a good man's heart, / One tear from a good man's eye'; one of the gamesters has a flash of conscience as they play, and then himself dies also, but they are all presented as utter scoundrels.[37]

In some versions of the tale, the body is disinterred by the man's friends; in others, it is already in the church, awaiting burial. Whichever version is told, and whatever inflection it is given, the tale is inherently intriguing: it blends understandable mourning with unconscionable sin.

[1] Reverend George Oliver, *History of the Holy Trinity Guild at Sleaford* (1837), quoted in Eliza Gutch and Mabel Peacock, *Examples of Printed Folk-Lore Concerning Lincolnshire* (David Nutt, 1908), p. 330.

[2] Adrian Gray, *Tales of Old Lincolnshire* (Countryside Books, 1990), p. 97.

[3] David Clark, *It Happened in Lincolnshire* (Merlin Unwin, 2016), p. 22.

[4] Ethel H. Rudkin, *Lincolnshire Folklore* (1936) (EP Publishing, 1973), p. 56.

[5] Irene Harris told Alison Brackenbury, by email in 2024, that a former head teacher at the village school, Bert Acum, would take his pupils to 'Gibbery Gap', then recite this rhyme.

[6] Ethel H. Rudkin, *The Diary of Ethel H. Rudkin: 1912-1930* (Old Chapel Lane Books, 2002), p. 40; Ethel H. Rudkin, *The Diary of Ethel H. Rudkin: 1935-1984* (Old Chapel Lane Books, 2002), p. 94.

[7] Rudkin, *Lincolnshire Folklore*, pp. 90-97.

[8] Marion Gibson, *Early Modern Witches: Witchcraft Cases in Contemporary Writing* (Routledge, 2000), pp. 276-98.

[9] Arnold Frost, *The Wind, the Devil, and Lincoln Minster: A Lincolnshire Legend* (1897), second edition (Boots, 1898).

[10] James Alpass Penny, *More Folklore Round Horncastle* (K. W. Morton, 1922), pp. 29-31; Mary Borrows, 'Witches in Lincolnshire', *Lincolnshire Life* (April, 1986), pp. 36-7, at p. 36.

[11] Susanna O'Neill, *Folklore of Lincolnshire* (History Press, 2012), pp. 115-30.

[12] Paweł Rutkowski, 'Animal Transformation in Early Modern English Witchcraft Pamphlets', *Anglica: An International Journal of English Studies* 28.1, pp.21-34.

[13] Bede, *Bede's Ecclesiastical History of England* (c.731), ed. A. M. Sellar (George Bell, 1907), p. 157-9.

[14] Rudkin, *Lincolnshire Folklore*, p. 32.

[15] Jacqueline Simpson and Steve Roud, *A Dictionary of English Folklore* (Oxford University Press, 2000), p. 37.

[16] Mabel Peacock, 'Folklore of Lincolnshire', *Folklore* 12.2 (1901), pp. 161-80, at p. 170.

[17] Maureen James, *Lincolnshire Folk Tales* (History Press, 2013), p. 83.

[18] Rudkin, *Lincolnshire Folklore*, pp. 58-61.

[19] 'A Lincolnshire Ghost: Supposed Discovery of Human Bones', *Illustrated Police News* (4 September 1897), p. 8.

[20] James John Hissey, *Over Fen and Wold* (Macmillan, 1898), pp. 288-95.

[21] Simpson and Roud, pp. 211-12.

[22] Marie Clothilde Balfour, 'Legends of the Cars', *Folklore* 2.2 (1891), pp. 145-170, at p. 155.

[23] Darwin Horn, 'Tiddy Mun's Curse and the Ecological Consequences of Land Reclamation', *Folklore* 98.1 (1987), pp. 11-15.

[24] George Hall, *The Gypsy's Parson: His Experiences and Adventures* (Sampson, Low and Marston, 1915) , pp. 38-40.

[25] Incident recorded in, for example, *Saint James's Chronicle* and *London Evening Post* (4 June 1811), p. 1. This variant of the rhyme is recorded in S. O. Addy, *Household Tales* (1895), p. 10, quoted in Gutch and Peacock, p. 353.

[26] A reliable, well-researched outline of events, and of Miller's influence on how they have been remembered, is Chris Hewis, 'Tom Otter: Fact or Folklore?', *Lincolnshire Past and Present* 93 (2013), pp. 13-16.

[27] Marie Clothilde Balfour, 'Legends of the Lincolnshire Cars - Part II', *Folklore* 2.3 (1891), pp. 257-283, at p. 277.

[28] Balfour, 'Legends of the Cars', p. 164.

[29] Katharine M. Briggs, *Folk Tales of Britain* (1970) (Folio Society, 2011), p. 194.

[30] Mabel Peacock, *Tales and Rhymes in the Lindsey Folk-Speech* (George Jackson, 1886), pp. 72-5.

[31] James, pp. 147-9, at p. 149.

[32] Joseph Jacobs, *English Fairy Tales* (David Nutt, 1890), pp. 148-151, at p. 151.

[33] Simon Young, *The Boggart Sourcebook* (Exeter University Press, 2022), p. vii.

[34] Young, p. 286.

[35] Daniel Codd, *Mysterious* (Breedon Books, 2007), p. 149.

[36] See Jim Moon, 'The Tale of the Holbeach Gamesters' (2023), South Holland Heritage <www.heritagesouthholland.co.uk/article/the-tale-of-the-holbeach-gamesters/> [accessed 23 August 2024]. An excerpt is included in James, *Lincolnshire Folk Tales*, p. 150.

[37] Phineas Garrett, ed., *100 Choice Selections, Number 25* (Penn Publishing, 1906), pp. 33-7, at p. 35.

BIOGRAPHICAL NOTES

Alison Brackenbury, born in Lincolnshire in 1953, is descended from long lines of servants and skilled farmworkers. She has published ten poetry collections, most recently *Thorpeness* (Carcanet, 2022) and *Gallop: Selected Poems* (Carcanet, 2019), and has broadcast frequently on BBC Radio 4. Alison is currently writing *Village*, a nonfiction prose book set in the extraordinary Lincolnshire village of her childhood.

Philippa East grew up in Scotland and originally studied Psychology and Philosophy at Oxford. After graduating, she moved to London to train as a Clinical Psychologist and worked in NHS mental health services for over a decade. Her debut novel, *Little White Lies*, was shortlisted for the CWA New Blood Dagger for best debut of 2020, and she has since published three psychological thrillers: *Safe and Sound*, *I'll Never Tell* and *A Guilty Secret*. For the last decade, Philippa has lived in Lincolnshire with her spouse and cat, where she continues to work as a psychologist and therapist.

Robert Etty was born and brought up in a village near Grimsby, and he has lived in or near Louth since 1975. For many years he worked as a teacher in a local secondary school. His poems first appeared in literary journals in the

1980s, and his most recent collection is *Beyond the Last House* (Shoestring, 2024).

John Gallas is a poet originally from Aotearoa, and the author of thirty-two books, mostly published by Carcanet Press. He spends a considerable amount of time in and around Holbeach Fen, where he has a little caravan on a farm near Sutton St James.

Fee Griffin is a Lincolnshire-based poet and lecturer. She is the author of *For Work/For TV* (Versal Editions, 2020) and *Really Not Really* (Broken Sleep, 2023), and won the Amsterdam Open Book Prize. Her poems have appeared in *Granta*, *Poetry London*, *The Rialto*, *Magma*, and elsewhere.

Rahul Gupta drew his first breath in Grimsby. He cherishes early memories of the town's grey sea and sky, of fighting his way, a little boy, along the seafront against the brutal wind, guzzling whelks and cockles in vinegar. Then he put a shell to his ear, and heard a poem. He lives in Lincolnshire.

Alex Harvey was born and raised in the Isle of Axholme, on the north-western edge of Lincolnshire, where he was brought up on stories and histories of his home, told by his grandmother Helen Beaumont and reinforced by his parents. Alex's passion for the past was chiselled through study at the University of York, and in 2023 he published an

Early Medieval history of the Isle of Axholme. He lives in York but revisits Lincolnshire frequently.

Juliet E. McKenna was born in Lincolnshire in 1965, and now lives in the Cotswolds. She has loved history, mythology and other worlds since she first learned to read. She has written twenty-five novels from *The Thief's Gamble* in 1999 to *The Green Man's Quarry*, winner of the BSFA Best Novel Award in 2023. Her varied shorter fiction includes horror, steampunk and science fiction.

Anna Milon obtained her PhD from the University of Exeter. Before joining the Lincolnshire Folk Tales Project as post-doctoral research fellow, she participated in a range of public outreach events, including loaning items and developing a series of seminars for the 'Fantasy: Realms of Imagination' exhibition at the British Library. She occasionally teaches Myths and Legends of the British Isles and the History of British Witchcraft and Magic at Advanced Studies in England, a study abroad programme based in Bath.

Daniele Pantano is a poet, essayist, literary translator, and artist. He has published over thirty books, and his work has been translated into a dozen languages and featured in various international journals. He lives in Lincoln and is Associate Professor in Creative Writing and Programme Leader for the MA and MFA Creative Writing programmes

at the University of Lincoln. His website is
www.pantano.ch.

Jane Simmons is a PhD student at the University of
Leicester. Her poems have appeared in various magazines,
have been shortlisted for a Candlestick Press prize (2023)
and placed third in the *Mslexia* poetry competition (2023).
She grew up in Lincoln and lives in a village close to
the city.

Nick Triplow is author of the crime novels *The Last Days of
Johnny Nunn*, *Never Walk Away* and *Frank's Wild Years*. His
biography of crime fiction pioneer Ted Lewis, *Getting Carter:
Ted Lewis and the Birth of Brit Noir*, was longlisted for the
CWA Gold Dagger for Non-Fiction and HRF Keating
Award. Nick is also the author of social history books *Pattie
Slappers*, *Distant Water*, and *The Women They Left Behind*.
Originally from London, he lives in Barton-upon-Humber.

Rory Waterman is the author of four collections of poetry
from Carcanet and was the editor of *Something Happens,
Sometimes Here, a collection of poetry by Lincolnshire poets*,
published by Five Leaves. He writes regularly for the literary
press, is the author of three critical books, and co-edits New
Walk Editions. Born in Belfast, he grew up just outside a
small village in North Kesteven, and now lives in
Nottingham, where he is Associate Professor of Modern and
Contemporary Literature at Nottingham Trent University.

Aliya Whiteley was born in Devon in 1974 and lived in Lincolnshire in the 1990s and 2000s while working as a library assistant. She writes strange stories and novels in the genres of science fiction, fantasy and horror. Her work has been shortlisted for both the Arthur C. Clarke award and Shirley Jackson award.

Anne Zouroudi is a true Yellowbelly, born in the village of Branston just outside Lincoln more years ago than she cares to count, into a family whose Lincolnshire credentials go back many generations. For much of her adult life she lived elsewhere, but in recent years she was drawn back, to the flatlands and big skies around Spalding.

Also Available From Five Leaves Publications

Something Happens, Sometimes Here
Poetry by Lincolnshire writers

Edited by Rory Waterman